# A ROYAL QUEST

A ROYAL QUEST.

# A
# ROYAL
# QUEST

## THE PRINCESS WARS

1

# MELODY CARLSON

*WhiteCrown*
PUBLISHING

This is a work of fiction. All characters and events portrayed in this novel are either fictitious or used fictitiously.

A ROYAL QUEST

WhiteCrown Publishing, a division of
WhiteFire Publishing
13607 Bedford Rd NE
Cumberland, MD 21502

ISBN: 979-8-88709-015-3 (print)
        979-8-88709-016-0 (digital)

# Once upon a time...

in the Kingdom of Raspen, twin princesses were born. The firstborn, and heir to the throne, was named Heather by the king. She debuted with a feisty spirit and blackened eye, rumored to have been given to her by her twin. The second princess, named Rose by the queen, emerged into the world wailing so loudly, some felt certain she was enraged over not being born first.

Over the years, the battles between the princesses continued. Some attributed the disturbing disputes to the untimely death of their mother. Deprived of the queen's gentle love and attention, the competition between the princesses increased. Although the girls were identical fair-haired beauties with topaz blue eyes and creamy complexions, no one ever confused one for the other.

Princess Rose believed she was "a princess's princess." She only wore the finest gowns and her hair ornately styled, followed by a cloud of her signature La Rosé perfume. But Princess Heather fancied the aroma of the horse stables and a riding habit over a frilly gown. She preferred books to baubles and would rather take up the sword than have her hair done.

Whether the topic was fashion or politics or even the weather, the princesses rarely agreed on anything. Their only commonality seemed to be a strong will that bordered on pigheadedness. And with their eighteenth birthday rapidly approaching and their elderly father failing, Princess Heather was on the cusp of being crowned Queen of Raspen, and Princess Rose was in a royal snit.

## Chapter One

*Keep it short and sweet.* Heather knocked on the door to her sister's chambers. *Tell Rose the news and make a quiet exit.* But Heather had barely announced her plan to be gone a few days before Rose exploded into a rage.

"I cannot believe you'd do this to me." Princess Rose hurled a golden hairbrush through the air, narrowly missing her sister's head.

"I'll only be gone a short while. You won't even—"

"There's much to be done in preparation for our eighteenth birthday celebration. You can't just leave."

"I'll be back before you know it," Heather reassured her.

"Of course you'd run off like this. You are thoughtless and irresponsible. And utterly *despicable*." Rose's voice soared in anger, yet her head remained still while her hairdresser continued patiently styling the golden curls.

"I doubt you'll even notice my absence." Heather slid a foot backward, preparing to escape. "I'll be back in no time. Don't worry so much."

"You should worry more." Rose paused, checking her reflection in her jewel-encrusted mirror and pointing out a loose strand her handmaid had missed. "Why am I even surprised? You always go your own way."

"Why not enjoy my absence," Heather said lightly. "With no one to fight with, you'll have some peace and quiet."

Rose growled as the hairdresser secured a bejeweled band into her hair. "Careful with those hairpins, Alice. My head is not made of wood."

Suppressing the urge to dispute this point, Heather inched toward the door. No point in prolonging this sisterly fracas with a careless comment. Especially after delivering her announcement at a time when Rose was preoccupied with primping. Why it required three handmaids to do this each morning was a mystery. But it did provide a good distraction for a hasty getaway. One more step back—

"Freeze right there," Rose commanded, as if preparing to be the royal ruler of Raspen.

"What now, *dear* sister?" Heather inhaled slowly. She would not engage in full-blown conflict. Not because she wouldn't relish a good scrap with her silly sister, but because she'd promised a peaceful departure to Father. *Diplomacy begins at home.* He'd reminded her of those words just last night.

"What about our birthday plans?" Rose demanded. "Leaving me with all the work like this? Proving once more you're foolish and selfish and, as I've told our father again and again, unfit for the throne."

Heather refused to take the bait. Balling her fists behind her back, she pursed her lips. "Rose, you know as well as I do that the servants will do all the work. They'll see to all the party preparations. You won't lift a finger—"

"But all the last-minute decisions, important details…surely you—"

"*Rose!* Be grateful I'm gone. You'd only debate every decision." Heather reached behind, feeling the carved surface of the heavy door. She grasped the engraved doorknob.

Rose's pink lips curved into a somewhat devious half-smile. "Perhaps you're right, Heather. Maybe it is best for you to take your childish escapade. Although I still think you're a fool."

"Fine, I'll be on my way—"

"Not so fast. Surely Father does not approve of this nonsense." With every hair in perfect place, Rose gracefully stood, keeping her back to Heather but still locking eyes with her reflection.

"Father's fine with it." Heather slowly turned the doorknob.

Rose untied the corded sash of her purple velvet dressing robe. "Really? Our father has approved your ridiculous plan? I'll wager you haven't even told him. Taking advantage of his condition to do as you please?" The handmaids waited with garments in hand, ready to dress their princess.

Heather held her breath, mentally counting to ten before answering. "Father has given me his full blessing."

Rose turned so abruptly that a handmaid toppled backward. "Father agrees to your plans?" Rose seethed. "Father wishes for a royal princess to gallivant the countryside like a commoner?"

Heather nodded, opening the door behind her. "Excuse me. I need to go."

"Speaking of commoners." Still dressed in just chemise and

bloomers, Rose pointed to Heather's drab gray gown. "Please tell me you are not going to parade about the kingdom in that pitiful rag?"

Heather tried not to smile as she smoothed the skirt of her serviceable woolen gown. If only her fashion-obsessed sister knew what Heather truly intended to wear. That would instigate a full-blown battle that the whole kingdom would know about before midday.

"Why should that surprise me?" Rose feigned a bored yawn as her handmaid cinched her into a lace-trimmed corset. "Do as you must, silly girl. Let the villagers see what their future queen truly is made of. See what kind of person intends to rule over them." She laughed. "Perhaps the villagers will stage a revolt on my behalf. One can only hope."

Heather forced a tight smile.

"Or perhaps—" Rose's blue eyes twinkled with mischief— "you will be so caught up in your foolish romp that you'll be unable to make it back here in time for the coronation." She held out her arms as her handmaids slid a shimmering gown of lavender satin over her head. "And then I shall take my place as Queen of Raspen. Wouldn't that be something."

"Hope springs eternal." Heather stepped out the door. "See you in a few days."

Rose hurled a few more insults, and Heather held her tongue as she scurried down the hall. It was time to say goodbye to Father. That would be much easier…and harder.

## Chapter Two

Heather found her father, the highly respected King of Raspen, in his tattered dressing robe, seated in his shabby easy chair, on the terrace outside of his Royal Chambers. With his chin tilted upward, his face lit by the morning sunshine, he appeared healthy and confident—the way he'd looked before his health had deteriorated in the past few months. For a moment, she could almost imagine that he was well and whole, ready to rule his empire for another twenty years or more.

"What a lovely morning." Heather planted a kiss on his creased brow. "And it looks as if you've eaten most of your breakfast, Father. Good for you." She plucked a leftover strawberry from a crystal bowl and popped it into her mouth. "Are you feeling better today?"

"I am trying to be well." He frowned as he patted his chest. "I have heeded the Royal Physician's advice, taken his herbs and treatments. My primary goal is to last long enough to see my daughters' eighteenth birthday. And then, when the time is right, to place the crown upon your fair head."

"Oh, Father." She tried to keep her voice light. "Don't worry.

You'll be here to celebrate out birthday. You're going to get well soon. I just know it."

He looked out at the rolling fields, green with spring grass and wildflowers, but Heather could see his gaze was farther away. "I hope you are right, dear daughter."

"Of course I'm right." She patted his shoulder, wishing he didn't feel so frail beneath his robe. "Keep following the physician's directions and getting good food and sunshine, and by midsummer you will be your old self again." She was aware her father had been discussing his future with Sir Edward and the rest of the council, planning for when he was gone. But she never liked to hear of it.

"I know you don't want me to speak of this, Heather. But there is the chance you will be ruling as queen before you are twenty."

"Twenty is a long way off, Father. We have plenty of time to discuss this later." She knew, based on her lessons with Sir Edward, that her father was doing all in his power to prepare her for leadership. And that would happen...someday. But today, she wanted to be free. Still, he needed reassurance. "But just so you know, I will do my best when the time does come. You have taught me well, Father. And, hopefully, years from now, I will make you proud." She picked up another strawberry, examining it in the sunlight before biting into it.

A faint smile played on her father's lips. "I know you will make a fine queen, Heather. I can feel it in my tired old bones."

She sat down on the footstool beside him and, taking his pale, wrinkled hand in her own, she attempted to rub warmth and life back into it. Apparently, she was not going to get away without having this talk. Again. No one besides Heather and the Royal Physician—not even Rose—knew of the king's real condition or that his illness might be serious. Still, she refused to give up hope. She wasn't ready to be queen. She wanted Father to get better. She wanted to go riding with him again, to visit the archery range, to go on a hunt next fall.

"I want to believe you are right, Father—that I will make a good queen."

"Certainly you will. Sir Edward always brags about you, my child. You are his most promising pupil."

Heather controlled the urge to roll her eyes. Sir Edward had only three pupils, and one of them was Rose. The other was Sir Edward's son, twelve-year-old Luther. "Sir Edward is a good teacher and a wise advisor, but I still feel uncertain, Father. I'm not sure I'm ready to take your place—to rule Raspen the way it should be ruled." She wanted to add that she wasn't ready to stand up against the Royal Council. Sometimes she wondered if her father stood up to them enough. Especially when he was ill. But she wasn't about to mention that now.

"My worst fear, my daughter"—he let out a long, sad sigh—"is that I have not left you an easy kingdom to rule."

She tilted her head to one side as she gazed out beyond the terrace, out over the wall and toward the village where most of the residents seemed happy and peaceful. "What do you mean?"

"I fear I've been neglectful. It began when your mother passed away and grew worse when my health began to falter. I fear that I left too many of my duties to others."

"But that is why you have your Royal Council, Father.

Certainly they have cared for your concerns. After all, they are wise and learned men." She knew this was only partially true. Most of them had the kingdom's best interests at heart. Especially Sir Edward. But she didn't trust all the councilors.

"I'm not so sure I should tell you this." He lowered his voice. "I don't like to say it, Heather, but I am not convinced we can continue to trust the Royal Council."

"What are you saying?" She stared at him, curious if he were about to declare what she'd suspected for the past several months.

"I am saying that I've decided to remove two councilmen. I plan to see to it today."

"Two councilmen? Really?" Heather had a good hunch which two Father meant, but she wanted to hear him say it.

"My Council Head and the Royal Treasurer." He stared out the window, but his empty gaze wasn't taking in any of the view.

"Sir Rupert and Sir Barnaby." She grimaced. "That will not be easy, Father."

"I know…but it must be done—and before you become queen. I wish I'd done it sooner, my dear."

"Do you want me to remain here, Father? To stand by you when you make these announcements?"

"No!" He shook his head. "It will be better if you are not part of this, Heather. Best if you are far away. If Rupert and Barnaby wish to protest, and I fear they will, let their actions fall on my head."

"Are you certain?"

He nodded. "It strengthens my heart to know I will see to this nasty piece of business before you are crowned." He patted her hand. "I only hope that it is enough."

"Enough?"

"I'm not sure. It's possible that Rupert and Barnaby have poisoned others." He sighed. "I believe you can fully trust Sir Benjamin and Sir Gordon. They are both good men. And, of course, Sir Edward can be trusted implicitly. But as for the others, time will tell."

She was relieved that Father was this aware. And perhaps cleaning out some bad councilors would prove to be good medicine. Maybe this meant he was ready to rule with the authority of the throne.

"What I can say for certain, Heather, is that you must see with your own eyes, you must hear with your own ears, and you must think with your own mind."

"What else would I use, Father?"

He smiled sadly. "Yes, exactly. Although you have good council in Sir Edward. That is a reassurance."

"Perhaps Sir Edward would agree to become head of the Royal Council."

"That's an excellent idea." His smile brightened. "And that is why I feel the monarchy will be in good hands...when I am gone."

She squeezed his hand and looked into his eyes. "Father, you *must* hold on. And follow the physician's directions. I will need you to guide me, to prepare me for the day when I take the crown. In the meantime, I hope I can be of help to you...to rule our people together."

He just nodded, but his pale blue eyes looked doubtful and tired and worried.

"Maybe I should forget this trip," she said. "I won't go after all. The timing is all wrong, and—"

He shook his head again. "Your plan to explore our regions is a wise one, Heather. I will admit, I didn't think so at first. But I do want you out among our people. I want you to see and hear what is happening with the farmers and the tradesmen. In the villages and the towns."

"That's what I hope to do, Father."

He gazed out over the landscape. "I regret I did not do this myself. You have my blessing, dear child. Go on your journey." He placed his hand on her head. "This is my present for your eighteenth birthday. I hope you'll enjoy it. I pray it will help prepare you for the day you accept your royal responsibilities. Have a grand adventure." His eyes lit up, making him appear younger and healthier. Perhaps he was improving.

Heather grinned. "Thank you, Father. It will be the grand adventure I've looked forward to for so long."

"What did your sister say about it?"

Her smile faded. "What do you think she said?"

"Never mind that. We knew she wouldn't approve." He rubbed his whiskered chin with a thoughtful expression as he looked out over the gardens. "I still remember the day you two girls were born. Almost eighteen years ago, on a day much like today."

"Springtime was unseasonably warm," she filled in for him. How many times had she heard this story? "Both the heather and the roses were in bloom at the same time that year."

"That's right. I named you, my firstborn, for my favorite plant. The hardy and resilient heather that so bravely springs forth—sometimes even while the snow is still on the ground. You are my strong child, my Heather."

Heather nodded. "And Mother named Rose for her favorite flower."

The king gave a rueful smile. "A lovely bloom, the rose. But it has its thorns. And, as you know, your dear sister can be prickly too. I'm afraid she has never gotten over being the second born."

"Don't I know it." Heather grimaced.

"You understand that she envies you, don't you?"

"Envies me? She hates the way I live, Father. She thinks I'm unfashionable and unprincessly, and she's certain I will make a terrible queen."

He let out a quiet chuckle. "That's because Rose doesn't understand what's important in a ruler. She never has. That is why I'm so thankful you were the firstborn, Heather. You were born to rule Raspen."

"I will do my best, Father. In the meantime, I should go." She looked out to where the sun was moving higher in the eastern sky. "I hate to leave you, but I did promise Sir Edward that I'd meet him at the outer stables by midmorning, and it's getting late."

"Yes, yes, do not let me detain you with my old reminiscences." He reached into a pocket of his dressing gown and removed a golden ring with a large sapphire stone circled by diamonds. For as long as Heather could remember, Father had worn this ring. It was the Royal Ring of the Kingdom of Raspen. "This is for you, dear daughter."

"But it's your ring, Father." She stared at the gleaming stone.

He removed a gold chain from his pocket, carefully threading it through the ring. "This will be *your* ring from this day forward— for as long as you live and rule. Keep it with you at all times, my child. It is the sign of the kingdom and of my—"

"But, Father—"

"I insist. I do not want you to go on this journey without it, Heather. Do you understand me?"

She nodded. "Yes, Father."

"Tip your head toward me, Daughter."

She leaned forward, waiting as he slipped the sturdy chain around her head, feeling the heavy thud of the ring against her chest.

"Thank you, Father."

He lifted a trembling hand and pressed his finger against her forehead. "Bless you, Princess Heather. Take the authority of Raspen with you wherever you go."

"I will." There was a long silence as they both sat there in the sunshine. Heather looked away and blinked back her tears. She wanted to appear as strong as her father believed her to be, but at the same time, she felt like a little girl.

"Be careful out there," he said. "Heed the advice and warnings of Sir Edward. He has your best interest at heart. And I do recommend you appoint him Head of the Royal Council. He may be unwilling at first. The good man prefers his books to politics. But I'm sure you can convince him. Whatever his role, Sir Edward is to be depended upon. He's my dearest and oldest friend, and I entrust him with your life, my child."

She nodded. "Please, don't worry. I have great respect for Sir Edward. I'll heed his counsel as if it comes from your own lips."

Her father's eyes brightened. "I am glad to hear that young Luther is going on this expedition with you. For a boy of twelve, he has a fine head on his shoulders. Someday he will make a wise advisor on your Royal Council." His expression turned grim again. "Even in his youth, Luther would be far preferable to Rupert and Barnaby." He waved his hand. "But never you mind about all that. I will see to these changes before the sun goes down."

"Speaking of the sun." She peered at the sky again. The sun was already over the treetops. "I should be on my way."

"God go with you, Princess Heather."

She reached out to embrace him as she kissed him goodbye. And then, sensing he was as close to tears as she, Heather stood and turned away. Without looking back, she walked from the terrace and exited his chambers. She was barely down the hall when she was assaulted by waves of guilt.

Was she wrong to leave her father like this? His health was fragile, but perhaps dealing with those crooked councilors would make him feel stronger. More in control of his kingdom. Besides, Heather wanted to prove her sister wrong. This trip was *not* selfish. It was part of her education and an important preparation for the day she would rule Raspen.

In fact, this escapade was as much for Father—and for the kingdom—as for herself. And, really, what would be the harm in having a bit of fun along the way? Chances were, it would be her last time for such adventures.

# Chapter Three

Heather smiled as she passed by the guards and servants. Tossing out her usual greetings—comments on the fine weather and inquiries about their families' health—she made her way down the ornately decorated hall. Without even looking up, she could feel the eyes of her ancestors looking down on her from their framed portraits. Were their serious expressions a sign of their general disapproval, or, like Father had once suggested, were they all just suffering from toothaches and gout and the pressures of ruling?

Running her hand along the polished banister, she hurried up the beautifully carved staircase that led to the back chambers. Tiptoeing, she went past her sister's closed door. Rose probably was down at breakfast. Heather opened her own door, calling out a friendly "hello" as she entered her chambers, hoping for solitude. She poked around to find no servant lurking about, no one changing linens or cleaning. Convinced she was alone, she locked her door and removed the key.

With a growing sense of excitement similar to the first time Father had allowed her to use a real bow and arrow, she got down on her knees next to her bed and, reaching deeply into the darkness underneath, grasped the precious bundle and slid it out. Knowing that the maids seldom, if ever, cleaned that far beneath her bed, she had stashed it there a week ago. She hugged the parcel to her chest as she stood. Wrapped in plain brown fabric and tied with string, it looked innocent enough, but what was inside would have shocked the chambermaid.

Feeling like a kid on Christmas morning, Heather opened the bundle and, one by one, removed the items of clothing, arranging them on her bed as if assembling a dummy or a scarecrow. Once it was all laid out, she clasped her hand over her mouth to hold back her snickers. It almost appeared as if a strange man were lying on her bed. Of course, it was not a real man. But it did look scandalous.

Both Father and Sir Edward had accepted the idea that Heather would disguise herself as a peasant for this week's excursion. It had taken some persuading, but eventually they saw the sense in her plan. Touring the region dressed as a commoner would allow her liberty to move about unnoticed. And it would be safer. Everyone agreed upon this.

However, what her elders did not realize was that her peasant costume was not that of a village woman. That would be too confining, too limiting. Women, especially villagers, were not allowed the same freedoms as men. Females didn't ride astride a horse or carry swords. For those reasons, Heather had spent the past several weeks gathering the wardrobe of a young man. And it had not been easy.

Heather let out a giddy laugh as she peeled off her layers of clothes. Tossing her plain dress onto a chair, followed by petticoats, she remembered Rose's concerns. Oh, if her sister could see her tugging on the brown trousers! The rough woolen fabric felt strange and itchy against her legs, but the pants would provide warmth while she camped in the woods at night. She tucked the tails of a light blue linen shirt into the waist, and concealed Father's sapphire ring beneath the shirt's broad yoke. Then she fumbled to thread the thick leather belt through the many belt loops, cinching the trousers tightly as she fastened the sturdy brass buckle.

Enjoying the new freedom of these trousers, she danced a little jig across her carpet then returned to dressing. The heavy tweed vest would help disguise her feminine curves. She paused to examine her image in the mirror. Not bad. Thanks to her height and slender build, along with these clothes, she could easily pass for a young man.

Except for that long golden hair. Heather reached for the shears she'd pilfered from the kitchen yesterday. She'd never been fond of her hair or the time she wasted styling it. Unlike Rose, who wore her curly golden locks like a crown, Heather would not mind lopping hers off. Except for Father. He would be dismayed to see Heather shorn like a boy—especially at her birthday celebration next week. Just last week, Father had examined the gown she was expected to wear, and he'd asked the royal hairdresser to arrange her hair in a coiled bun. Like her mother used to wear. Heather set down the shears and reached for a hairbrush.

Brushing her curls as straight as possible, she divided her hair into two sections, which she plaited tightly and wrapped around her head, pinning them firmly into place like a skullcap. As she squinted at her reflection from a short distance, she could almost imagine she was a boy with short blond hair. But without a hat, the braids were clearly visible. She'd have to keep her hat on in public, but that shouldn't be too difficult. And this new hairstyle would certainly be easy to maintain during her big adventure. Imagine almost a week with no hairdressing!

Heather pulled the broad-brimmed brown felt hat onto her head, securing it with more hairpins. After giving her head several shakes, she was convinced that even during a bumpy trot, it would stay in place. Finally, she tugged on the tall black boots. She grinned to remember the story she'd told the cobbler more than a month ago when she handed him the pattern she'd traced of her foot. "A birthday present for a boy, someone we've grown quite fond of over the years," she told the old man. "They must be sturdy leather yet comfortable." The cobbler had assumed the boots were for Luther, and she did not correct him.

For the last time, she studied her image in the mirror. Pulling the hat down lower on her brow, she felt assured that no one would guess that this young man was a princess. Never. A bit of dust and grime might help her charade, but she was confident she could pass through the palace—perhaps even beneath her snooty sister's powdered nose—without being discovered. Pleased with her miraculous transformation, Heather gathered her spare boy clothes, a fresh shirt in a darker shade of blue and a few other necessities, and wrapped them inside a dark tartan cloak, which she rolled like a large sausage and secured with twine.

It was time to meet Sir Edward and Luther. But first she must exit her chambers without being observed. It wouldn't do for a young man to be spotted emerging from Princess Heather's sleeping quarters. She silently opened the door, peering up and down the hallway. As usual, it was quiet and deserted this time of day. Rose was still at breakfast, and the servants were starting morning chores.

With heart pounding, Heather stepped into the hallway and closed the door then approached the stairs. Seeing and hearing no one below, she hurried down. It wasn't until she was crossing the massive marbled floor in the main hall that someone took notice.

"What are you doing in here, young man?" The head maid shook a feather duster at Heather with a scowl. Eunice was an elderly servant, but her eyesight was fine. And she had known Heather since infancy.

"I took some quails to the kitchen," Heather said in a husky voice she'd rehearsed for a week. "For supper, mum." She tipped her head down as if self-conscious.

"Then why did you not take your leave through the servants' door?"

"I'm sorry, mum. Me and my brother, we caught a dozen fat quails this morning, and we knows the king loves quail. I was so eager to bring 'em, I didn't know which way to take. It's my first delivery to the palace, mum. I'm awful sorry." With a mixture of pride and guilt over her ability to fib so convincingly, she ducked her head in apology.

Eunice's tone softened. "That way with you, boy." She pointed toward the servants' entrance. "And mind your manners, or this might be your last delivery to the palace. You hear?"

"Much obliged, mum." Heather touched her hat and tipped

her head, scurrying toward the back of the palace. It had worked—
it had really worked! If she could fool someone who knew her, she
should be able to fool anyone. *Anyone!*

# Chapter Four

As Heather exited through the servants' entrance, she suppressed the urge to let out a victory whoop. This was going to be so much better than exploring as Princess Heather or even as a female villager. Pretending to be a boy was exhilarating! And brilliant! When she'd ventured out among the villagers as her usual royal self, *dressed* as a princess (albeit an unfashionable one), she was *treated* as a princess and probably only saw what was acceptable for a princess to see. Now it was like being invisible. She could wipe her nose with her shirt sleeve or let out a loud belch, and no one would notice.

Her goal was to witness the real condition of her father's monarchy—the good and the bad and everything in between. She wanted to experience the reality of the people she would soon rule. And, truth be told, she wanted to have a great adventure while she was at it. This costume would allow her to venture much farther than before.

She held her head high as she strolled, taking on the stance of a confident young man. She liked the clickety-click sound of the heels on her new boots echoing down the cobblestone street that led to the Royal Stables. *I am free. I am free. I am free.*

She imagined the freedom to explore the furthermost places. Like the Wilderness. All she knew was that it was dangerous, untamed land beyond the Borderlands. Wouldn't it be grand to see it? Had anyone from the Royal Family ever been there? Father had told her it was too dangerous to visit.

She glanced at the tall wall that encompassed the palace grounds. Constructed of massive granite stones, it loomed twenty feet high and was thicker than the width of her father's arm. "The wall is to protect you," her father had told his daughters often enough. Rose had always accepted this as fact. With no interest in going beyond the wall, Rose was fearful the few times Father had taken them into Southside. If a villager came too close, Rose grew agitated, demanding to return home at once.

Although Heather respected the secure wall, she'd always felt its restrictions. From an early age, she'd longed to get beyond it. When she was old enough, she began to sneak out whenever possible. But she'd never been satisfied, never seen enough.

Only seven days remained until her birthday, and she was aware she might spend the rest of her life cooped up within the palace walls. With the fate of the kingdom weighing heavily upon her shoulders, the responsibility to rule and reign, she would be confined to endless planning meetings and council sessions. She would be expected to cooperate with all the fussy pomp and circumstance connected to her responsibilities. All within the confine of the well-guarded palace walls. But today she was young and free, and her great adventure was about to begin!

When Heather reached the stables, she could tell her friends were concerned about her whereabouts. Peering up and down the alley, their faces were clouded with worry. But neither of them paid her much heed as she strolled right past them. So she walked by again. Then, pausing in the shadows, she leaned against her horse's stall and whistled to herself. Pretending to be occupied by the tie on her bundle, she listened to their conversation.

"I cannot imagine what's keeping her," Sir Edward said, his brow furrowed. "She was excited about today. She wanted an early start."

"And she's not usually late." Luther looked over his shoulder again. His eyes skimmed Heather with a suspicious expression, and he lowered his voice. "Do you think something went wrong? Perhaps, uh…" He glanced her way again. Did he suspect she was eavesdropping? "Perhaps they decided it was too dangerous. The plan was changed?"

"If that were true, I would have been informed." Sir Edward stroked his gray-tinged beard the way he always did when troubled.

Heather turned away, concealing her amusement and controlling her giggles. They did not recognize her. The costume was a success. When she could stand it no longer, she spoke out.

"Here I am." She stepped into the sunshine, squaring her shoulders with a wide grin.

Sir Edward peered at her. "Did you say something, young man?"

"It is I, Sir Edward." She bowed deeply but did not remove her hat. "Princess Heather," she said in a hushed tone, just in case someone was listening.

Sir Edward's eyes widened before he blinked and blinked again.

"Princess Heather?" Luther leaned forward to gape at her. "Is it really you?"

She nodded. "But do not call me by that name. From now on—at least for the duration of this journey—I am to be known as Harry."

Luther stood up straight and grinned. "Whatever you say, Harry." He chuckled at his attempt at humor. "At your service, Harry."

"Princess Heather," Sir Edward exclaimed, using the same tone he resorted to when his pupils were disorderly.

"Please!" Heather glanced around in concern that someone might overhear them. "The name is Harry."

"I do not understand, uh, Harry." Sir Edward shook his head. "Whatever has possessed you to dress like a—"

"It's my disguise. So I can pass freely among my people." She pointed to her horse. As expected, her trustworthy steed was already outfitted in her clumsy sidesaddle. "Please remove *that* from Zephyr. I wish to ride with a normal saddle."

"I'll change it for you," Luther offered.

"And do not fetch me a Royal Saddle," she warned him. "No insignias or gold. Just a plain and simple seat, please."

"I know just the one." Luther grinned as he undid the cinch of the bulky saddle. "This trip is going to be interesting."

"You are right about that," she proclaimed in her masculine voice. "We will be three explorers out to see the world. It will be *very* interesting. And, I hope, fun too."

Sir Edward did not look convinced. "But Princess—"

"Harry," she hissed, shaking her finger under Sir Edward's long, pointed nose, prepared to pull rank if necessary.

He nodded. "Tell me, *Harry*, how does King Reginald feel about the masquerade game you are playing?"

"The king is in favor of my going incognito," she assured him. Of course, she didn't mention her father assumed she would be visiting the village as a peasant woman, not a man. But, really, what her father didn't know wouldn't hurt him.

"I think it's a splendid plan." Luther hoisted the replacement saddle onto Zephyr's shiny brown back. "Heath—I mean Harry—will be able to see a lot more as, well, as Harry."

"Precisely." Heather was relieved that Luther supported her in this, and as he adjusted the cinch, she secured her clothes bundle behind the saddle. "And because Zephyr isn't a flashy sort of horse, I don't expect him to be recognizable."

Sir Edward turned his attention to his horse's bridle. "I suppose I am beginning to see the sense of your idea. Truth be told, I had my concerns about the appearance of Luther and myself in the company of a young villager woman. Tongues were apt to flap over that. And if the news made its way back to Luther's mother, well, I might find myself in hot water by the time we get home."

"Or sleeping in the woodshed," Luther teased.

"You see," Heather told Sir Edward, "it is a perfect plan."

"Time will tell," Sir Edward answered.

"There." Luther slapped the top of the sleek leather saddle. "Zephyr is ready to ride."

Heather smoothed her hand over Zephyr's sleek, dark mane.

"I'll bet you like this saddle much better, don't you, boy? Much lighter."

"Is the pack horse ready?" Sir Edward asked his son.

"Almost." Luther tightened the cinch then tested the strength of the ropes securing their food and camp supplies. "Give me two shakes of a lamb's tail."

"Thank you for understanding," Heather whispered to Sir Edward while they waited for Luther. "I felt certain you would see my rationale."

"I see your rationale, but..." His gray eyes flickered with concern. "I do not take my responsibilities lightly." He glanced over his shoulder and lowered his voice. "You're heir to the throne. My primary job is to *protect* you, and, believe me, it will be no small task...Harry."

"I know. And for that I am most grateful." Without any assistance, Heather slipped her foot into the stirrup and in one swift motion seated herself in the saddle. Riding astride would be so much easier. Sometimes she wondered if men hadn't dreamt up sidesaddles just to make life harder on women. She pointed at Luther as he led out the packhorse. "You have my things? My bow and arrow? My sword? My knife?"

"You will not need those things," Sir Edward reminded her.

"I haven't spent years of lessons with these tools of defense only to leave them behind."

"Don't worry," Luther assured her. "It's all here, Harry."

"Along with everything else we need for our journey." Sir Edward lifted his foot to the stirrup.

And with no fanfare or trumpet blasts, the three riders,

followed by the loaded packhorse, began their journey. Heather felt the thrilling rush of independence as they exited the palace gates, clomping over the heavy wooden drawbridge then down into the village of Southside. Their plan—Heather knew because she had made it—was not to tarry here in this charming little village nestled so close to the palace.

Heather had been forbidden to travel beyond Southside before. Not that she'd always obeyed this restriction. But today was about freedom and adventure.

## Chapter Five

As they walked their horses through Southside, familiar shops and thatched houses came into view. This was an attractive and well-maintained village. As usual, the structures appeared freshly whitewashed, the doors were prettily painted, and the flowerboxes overflowed with colorful blooms. The cobblestone streets were swept neatly and the doorsteps were scrubbed. Even the villagers looked clean and neat, smiling respectfully as they greeted Sir Edward and his son without suspecting that their traveling companion was their princess.

Like always, the insinuation here was that all was well. The image of goodness and light. Yet Heather had suspected for almost a year that this was not the complete picture. Sometimes while visiting Southside, she'd caught snippets of conversations. Words that suggested people were not as contented as she'd presumed. She suspected the villagers were putting on a show for the palace, which was troubling. She hoped that her disguise would aid in putting these pretenses aside. She longed to see the villagers for who they truly were, not an act for royals.

But Southside and Westside were different. She'd seen it with her own eyes when, not long ago and without having asked

Father's permission, Heather had ventured to Westside. She'd never understood why Father had forbidden her to go there, but it hadn't taken long to discover that Westside was much shabbier than Southside. She'd been dismayed to find the small, unkempt houses in disrepair. And the muddy main road, flanked by a few uninviting shops, hadn't even had cobblestones. She'd even peeked through a grimy shop window to spy barren shelves. The general impression had been one of poverty. Sadness.

But it was the villagers that had haunted her most. Not because of their ragged, patched clothes and dirty, bare feet but because of their unfriendly scowls as she'd ridden her horse through their village. They had recognized the princess, yet they'd seemed openly hostile. Some even told her to go away. And she hadn't lingered. Back at the palace, she'd confessed her visit to Father, but this information seemed to make his precarious health worsen. She'd kept her concerns to herself. But now she hoped to get to the bottom of it.

The three travelers stopped for a midday meal a short way out of Southside. As they dined on cheese and bread and fruit, Heather reminded Sir Edward of her concerns about Westside.

"Yes, I remember you told me of your visit." He broke a piece of bread.

"And you told me of your disapproval," she said.

"It's not a safe place for a princess to travel alone."

"Which is why I'm so glad to be in your company." She smiled then sighed. "As much as I want this to be a great adventure, I must admit I am worried about the kingdom. I know my father is worried too."

"For good reason." He nodded somberly.

"I suspect there is much more beneath the surface in our villages."

"What do you mean?" Luther asked.

"I know that villagers act differently when royalty rides through their streets. I've seen it before. But today was different." Heather remembered some of the candid scowls and narrowed eyes she'd observed. "I see that all is not well. There are poverty and ill feelings. I can't really explain it, and I'm not sure of the source of these troubles, but I know they exist. And I'd like to get to the bottom of it if I can."

"Which is why you will be a good ruler when the time comes," Sir Edward told her.

"That's what my father keeps telling me, but I'm not as confident as he."

"Perhaps your lack of confidence will help you." Sir Edward cut off a wedge of cheese.

"How can that be?" Luther asked.

"Humility can be a good teacher. A certain kind of lowliness can make a person question and look deeper. Like Princess Heather is doing today."

"You mean *Harry*," Luther reminded with a twinkle in his eye.

"Yes. Harry," Sir Edward corrected.

"What you said about humility," Heather pressed him. "Do you really think that's true? Sometimes I worry that Father has been too lowly. He's let some of his councilmen run roughshod right over him."

Sir Edward nodded without speaking.

"You know Father is dismissing two councilmen today?"

He nodded again.

"Who is he getting rid of?" Luther asked eagerly. "I bet I know." But before he could say, his father spoke.

"Rupert and Barnaby. I am grateful not to be in that meeting today. I am assured of the other councilmen. Gordon and Benjamin are in full support of King Reginald. I believe Rolland and Stewart are as well. But it is time for change."

"Will that be up to you someday?" Luther asked Heather. "Will you help to bring about changes?"

Heather looked nervously at Sir Edward. "When the time comes. I hope I'll have help and guidance."

"Let's not worry about that now." Sir Edward stood. "Your father wants you to enjoy your adventure, Princess Heather."

"You mean Harry," Luther corrected again.

Sir Edward smiled. "So let us enjoy our adventure. Even if it becomes uncomfortable."

"Why uncomfortable?" Luther asked.

"Having one's eyes opened can hurt at times." Sir Edward began to bundle their leftover food. "But in the end, it is for the best." He stood. "We have a three-hour ride ahead. We should get going."

"On to Harry's great adventure." Luther grabbed the knapsack of food and tied it onto the pack horse.

Heather laughed as she climbed into the saddle. *Harry's Great Adventure.* It sounded like the title of an exciting book. Perhaps she'd write about it someday.

Heather was grateful conversation had lulled by the time the trio traveled through the countryside. The quiet allowed her to take everything in. She wanted to study the lay of the land, observing how the village neighborhoods gave way to land used for agriculture. Freshly planted fields of cabbages and corn and wheat grew lush and colorful, promising plentiful food by harvest time. She spied occasional farm workers going about their chores.

Beyond the bucolic farmland lay gently rolling hills and meadows, bright green grassy slopes where sheep, goats, cows, and an occasional horse grazed. She had studied geography with Sir Edward, so she knew that beyond the hills lay the rugged, forested country of the Borderlands, where deer and wild boar were hunted, and beyond that lay the Wilderness.

She breathed in the fresh spring air, squinting up into the clear blue sky. It was all beautiful, especially this time of year. She was proud to think that this was just one part of the Raspen dominion and that someday she would be queen of all she could see. But for today, she was just Harry.

As they rode west, she dreamed of the other regions they would explore. She hoped they would make Northside by evening. She had no idea what they'd find there, but she was eager to see everything in their kingdom. It had always felt large and mysterious before. But today all was wide open and welcoming, and she felt no guilt for sneaking out without permission. And being dressed like this not only made riding much easier but was liberating. As if she were in control of her destiny and her whole world.

Heather spotted Westside on the horizon, perhaps a mile or two beyond a green meadow and what looked like a freshly planted cornfield. She was glad that they would only pass by the outskirts of that village. Her travel plan had not included another visit to Westside today. Not because she'd felt uncomfortable there before. She was confident her disguise would take care of that. But she'd already seen enough of this region and didn't care to waste precious time here when there was so much more to see beyond it.

Her route, clearly marked on her map, traveled the perimeter of the village then headed directly north. Since Northside was the farthest region in the Kingdom of Raspen, she estimated it would take a full day of travel just to reach the forest nearby. But it was the place she'd been most curious about for some time, and she was eager to see it firsthand.

But it looked like Sir Edward had a different plan. "You appear to be heading directly toward Westside," she said as she reined in her horse next to his. "I thought you knew of my plans."

"Forgive me, Princess—"

"Harry!" Luther called out from behind them.

"Yes, well, Harry. I think that because of our late start today, we should make a change in the plan. We cannot expect to make it all the way to Northside before dark."

"But why not just travel as far as we can go then stop?"

"I have decided it is better for us to stop in Westside for the night. We will stay at the Westside Village Inn."

"The village inn?" Disappointment washed over Heather. Already her big adventure felt diminished. "I thought we were going to camp overnight in the woods."

"For our first night, we should stay indoors." Sir Edward turned his horse onto the right fork of the road and headed westward.

"I do not agree with your decision," she said sharply.

"I thought you wished to see how the people lived."

"I do. But I have been to Westside before."

"And what did you see? What beyond the surface did you experience? You said they treated you poorly because they knew you were Princess Heather."

She considered this. "That's true."

"Why not mix with the villagers as one of them?" Sir Edward asked.

"We are certain to meet some colorful people at the village inn," Luther pointed out. Had his father coached him?

"Luther is right. Staying in an inn is a rare opportunity for royalty. You will see your subjects in a new light."

"Perhaps you're right, Sir Edward. Besides, there will be plenty of opportunities to sleep under the stars before we go home."

"I look forward to it. And be warned that I plan to test my pupils on the constellations when we camp." He nodded toward Luther. "Both of you."

# Chapter Six

About a mile from Westside, the landscape was not as lush and green and pretty as the land around Southside and surrounding the palace. The rutted road was much dustier. With no farms nearby, this stretch of country was desolate and neglected. As if it had been left behind. Was it because of the climate? Or was something more going on?

The sun dipped low on the horizon as Heather and her companions continued riding. They must've been moving more slowly than she'd estimated in her plan because she'd hoped to be farther by now. Her late start had cost them valuable travel time.

"Looks like another traveling party up there." Heather pointed to the small brown cloud not far ahead.

"I noticed." Sir Edward fingered his beard. "We would have less dust if we slowed our pace, but if we do that, we may not make it to the inn before dark."

"Let's gallop and pass them," Luther suggested.

"Gallop our horses?" Heather thought that sounded fun.

"Then they can eat our dust," the twelve-year-old declared. "Surely the king's horses are faster than their old nags."

Sir Edward gave Luther an exasperated look. "Think about it, son. How may those travelers behave if we race in front of them like that? What may they do if we showered them with our dust?"

Heather knew that Sir Edward wanted to turn this into a lesson. "Your father's right," she said. "And there are more of them than us. And they may not be friendly."

"But they have to treat you with respect," Luther reminded her. "You are a princess."

"But they won't know that. To them I am just *Harry*, remember? And for all we know, they could be a band of thieves."

"Or just old men on old horses." Luther gave her a daring look as he kneed his horse into a gallop. But after a few seconds, he stopped, turning to grin mischievously at them.

"Silly boy." Sir Edward shook his head.

"He just wants to have a little fun." Heather poked Sir Edward in the arm. "A great adventure. I can understand that."

"But you do not have to *create* your adventure. Trust in fate… and give it time. I'm certain your adventure will create itself."

The sun had sunk below the treetops by the time they reached the two-story inn. As she dismounted her horse, Heather saw that the other travelers, the ones who had made their ride so dusty, were only a pair of men, and they were going into the inn. As she led her horse to the nearby stable where Luther was waiting, she was relieved to know she would have a bed to sleep in tonight. Even though the standard saddle was more comfortable than a sidesaddle, she was stiff and sore, and the wool fabric of her trousers had worn hot patches on the insides of her legs. She needed to toughen up.

"Luther will tend to your horse," Sir Edward told her as she dismounted. "Take only what you need for the night."

"What about the packhorse?" She untied her bundle of spare clothes. "Will our valuables be safe from thieves?"

Sir Edward removed a money bag from the packhorse. "I'll take the valuables in with us."

Heather knew her father was funding their excursion. He had shown her the bag yesterday.

"And I will bring the bag holding your weapons," Luther promised.

Sir Edward handed Luther some coins. "Pay the stable hand extra to ensure that our supplies are secure for the night."

"The inn looks busy," Heather observed as they made their way to the tall stone building. She could hear voices and laughter, and, through the yellow light of the windows, she saw people moving about inside.

"I hope they have rooms." Sir Edward pushed open the door.

Heather felt a rush of excitement as they entered the warm, smoky room. People, mostly men, were seated at rough hewn tables lit by kerosene lamps. The back wall, made of stacked stones, had a fireplace with a small fire smoldering. But it was the smell that gave her pause—a pungent aroma of unwashed bodies, cooking smells, and some other foul odor. Maybe just the fragrance of too many humans inhabiting a relatively small space.

"We have arrived from Southside and require two rooms," Sir Edward informed the innkeeper. "There are three of us."

"You're out of luck. I just gave out the last two rooms." The innkeeper jerked his thumb to a couple of men sitting down at a table.

"The travelers on the road ahead of us," Heather said in a deep voice. Perhaps Luther's idea to overtake them had been a good one after all.

"Two rooms for only the two men?" Sir Edward queried. "Perhaps they can share a room and we can have the other? Or perhaps, *for the right price*, you would like to give us both rooms?"

"And what about them two?" The innkeeper frowned at the men oblivious to the discussion.

Heather turned to study the interlopers who had not only coated her traveling party with dust but had taken the last rooms in the inn. The younger one had dark, curly hair and a strong profile. He didn't appear much older than she. His companion looked older. Perhaps they were father and son. The two were dressed neatly—not covered in dust—and they didn't appear to be troublemakers, but one never knew.

Sir Edward held out his hand to the innkeeper, exposing two gold coins worth far more than the cost of all the rooms for several nights. "Perhaps this will change your mind, good sir."

The innkeeper's eyes widened. "Let me see what I can do."

Heather watched as the stocky bald man walked to the table where the two men were seated and bent over to speak to them. The young man looked up with intense brown eyes, shaking his head no. "We already paid you for our rooms," he said. "You can't just take them back like that."

"I can if I want," the innkeeper declared.

"That's wrong, and you know it," the young man said calmly.

"It's *my* inn, and I run it the way I like. Either give up your rooms, and I'll return your money." He lifted a doubled fist. "Or I'll throw you both out, and I'll keep your money. Your choice."

The young man looked over to where Heather and Sir Edward were waiting, studying them as if they were the source of his troubles. Maybe they were. Then he stood with a frown. "I only see two men," he told the innkeeper. "Why must *they* have two rooms?" He strolled over, studying Sir Edward and Heather. Surely he did not intend to fight. With his height and size, he would have the advantage.

"Can we not agree upon a compromise?" He directed this to Sir Edward. "You fellows take one room, and we'll take the other, and everyone will have a place to sleep tonight? After all, there are only two of you." He smirked at Heather. "And just *barely* two, young man."

Heather's hackles rose as she glared at him. "There are *three* of us. Our other traveling companion is tending to the horses."

"Yes, fine, but we were here first and already have secured the—"

"As the innkeeper said, it's his inn to run as he pleases." She squared her shoulders.

"Does that make it right for him to turn us out after we've already paid for two rooms?"

She shrugged. He had a point, but her backside was throbbing, and she didn't care for his impertinence.

He gave an amused grin. "You're a rather slight fellow. I doubt you take up much space in a bed. There should be room for three.

You and your friends take one room, and we'll take the other." He stuck out his hand as if he expected her to shake it.

His suggestion that she share a bed with Sir Edward and Luther irked her even more. If this brazen young man knew he was talking to his future queen, he would be mortified. However, she could not reveal this. And so she rejected his hand, folding her arms across her chest as she glared at him.

"If we can reach an agreement," he continued, "you can inform the innkeeper that we are happy to give up one of our rooms. It won't be as comfortable, but that is a concession we can—"

"I already told you"—the innkeeper put his round, ruddy face close to the young man's—"your rooms are taken. You can go quietly, and I'll give you your money back. Or you can make a fuss, and I'll throw you out and keep your blooming money."

The young man looked flustered but not frightened. He held his ground, staring down the innkeeper. "You, sir, are not running a fair establishment, and I—"

"I warned you," the innkeeper growled. "Go quietly, or I'll have you tossed out on your ear."

Sir Edward glanced at Heather as if he wanted her to resolve this squabble. How many times had he lectured her on diplomacy and peacemaking? Perhaps this was just another test of her leadership skills. Certainly, it would be easy to get her way and have her own private room since the innkeeper, thanks to the gold coins, was on their side. But seeing the young man's understandable frustration, she felt torn. Did she really want to be that selfish? Sure, she was soon to be queen and had every right to demand her way, but was that how the future monarch should act? If she were her sister, there would be no question. And to be honest, she would rather enjoy watching the innkeeper throw out this uppity young man. On the other hand, that was wrong. Besides, he was not unattractive. And other than the comment about her stature, which was true, he had been polite.

"We would like to make a compromise," she told the innkeeper, as if it were her own idea. "Our party will only require one room. Let these men keep the other."

The innkeeper looked at Sir Edward in disappointment. "But you offered to pay for *two* rooms." It was obvious he wanted both gold coins in Sir Edward's hand, and he was more than willing to throw out the other men to get them.

"Here you go, my good man." Sir Edward dropped one gold coin in his hand with a warm smile. "Keep the change. And we need meals for three of us. Thank you."

The innkeeper grumbled as he pocketed the coin and turned away. Never mind that it was far more than one room was worth. Greed left to itself was not pretty.

"Thank you for willingness to compromise." The younger man winked at Heather. "For someone who's still wet behind the ears, you've got a good head on your shoulders."

"Do not mention it." Not accustomed to such disrespect, she held her head high, attempting to act nonchalant. If nothing else, she reminded herself, this experience could be good practice. Several days of eating humble pie might not be as easy as she had anticipated.

The young man's smile was laced with superiority as he placed a careless hand on her shoulder. "And since we're letting bygones be bygones, would you fellows care to join us for supper? My name is Michael, and this is Sir Jonathan. We're journeying to Southside. Did we hear you say that you hail from those parts?"

"That's right," Heather answered.

"We left there this morning. Where are you fellows from?" Sir Edward asked in a friendly tone, but the glint of his eyes hinted that he was more than just curious.

"Well, we're not from Raspen." Michael studied Heather, removing his hand from her shoulder.

Sir Edward nodded. "No, I thought not."

"So, we are all travelers tonight. Please, join us for supper," Michael urged.

"No, thank you." Heather shook her head. She'd had enough of his condescension.

"Then let us buy you a pint of ale."

Sir Edward looked at Heather, but once again she shook her head no.

"I'm sorry," Sir Edward told him. "Pleasant journey to you."

Michael's eyes flickered with offense but quickly transformed into indifference. Without saying another word, he turned on his heel and strutted off in a way that Heather could not help but categorize as arrogance. Then, as if to confirm her opinion, he murmured something to his companion, and they both laughed loudly, as if they were enjoying some unkind joke. Probably at Heather's expense.

"Some people have no upbringing," she whispered to Sir Edward. "No manners whatsoever."

"Sometimes one's manners are reflective of one's company."

Sir Edward averted his eyes as he waved to Luther, who was just entering the building.

"And to think I spared those rude men from being thrown out of here," she seethed. "Perhaps that was a mistake."

"One should never regret an act of graciousness, uh—" He paused as if catching himself from calling her Princess Heather. "Harry." He rubbed his beard as he gave her one of his stern tutor's expressions.

Glancing away from him, she looked over to where the two men were still amused over something. Perhaps she was being thin-skinned, but she suspected it was her. They probably were chuckling over the way Michael had put her down. But when the surly young man looked over, directly into her eyes, his smile seemed innocent and genuine. And as she turned away with flushed cheeks, she couldn't help but admit to herself that, for a commoner, Michael was nice looking.

## Chapter Seven

It wasn't long until their meal was served: a generous chunk of fatty beef with boiled potatoes, turnips, and bread. Although it was nothing like what would be served in the palace tonight, Heather was famished. As she cleaned her plate, she watched and listened to the various guests at the inn. Some were a bit rough around the edges and probably not to be trusted, but others, including a tinker and a scholar and an artisan, were interesting company.

However, she realized that most were "just passing through," and learned little about the region of Westside. One commonality she surmised from nearly everyone she spoke with—no one seemed particularly fond of Raspen royalty or the general leadership stemming from the palace. Some were downright hostile. It was more than a little concerning.

They were finishing their meal when a flamboyant young woman wearing a feathered hat and an emerald-green gown trimmed with bands of purple entered the inn. At first, Heather wondered if she might be a gypsy. She had never seen anyone like her before, and she was curious to find out more. She'd heard that gypsies occasionally roamed through Raspen. However, as the woman strolled in, greeting the guests and going to the innkeeper, Heather decided she wasn't a gypsy. For a moment, Heather thought she might be a lady—albeit a colorful one. She was an eye-catcher, and most of the eyes in the room turned to watch as she spoke to the innkeeper. They exchanged words as if they were well-acquainted, but she seemed too young to be his wife. Perhaps she was his daughter.

The young woman glanced around the room, and her eyes settled on the table where Heather, Luther, and Sir Edward were seated, almost as if she wanted to join them. Heather gave her a cautious smile. The woman bustled over, smiling as she invited herself to sit down.

"I see you are strangers to our region." She looked at Heather with keen interest. The woman's gown was tattered and worn and soiled, and her lips and cheeks were artificially reddened.

"Yes." Heather remembered to use her manly voice. "We're passing through from Southside."

"Ah." The woman's eyes, the same color as the gown, sparkled as she smiled. "My name is Bess. I welcome you to Westside. We may not be as fancy as them folks in Southside, but we're friendly enough, we are." She reached over, stroking Heather's arm in an overly familiar way.

"Thank you. I'm Harry." Heather pulled away her arm and introduced her companions.

"Harry." Bess fluttered her lashes. "A fine name for a fine young man."

Heather cleared her throat, glancing at Sir Edward, who looked rather amused. "Yes, well, now that we've finished our meal, I suppose we should call it a day. Long day of travel ahead."

"Oh, Harry," Bess murmured as she inched closer to Heather on the wooden bench. "Don't you be leaving so soon, my friend. I want the pleasure of knowing you better." She slid her arm around Heather's shoulders with a twittering laugh. "You're so handsome, and the night is young."

Heather jerked away as the realization hit her. This woman was flirting with her. "I'm sure it would be good to know you better." She forced a nervous smile. "But I fear I must decline."

Bess frowned but, without missing a beat, focused her attentions on Sir Edward. "Well, you're a fine-looking old fellow, you are. How would you like to get to know Bess better?" She reached over to finger his beard.

Sir Edward blinked in surprise as he pulled his head back. "No. Thank. You." He turned to Luther. "My son and I are about to turn in. It's been a rather wearying day."

Bess's brow creased as she stood. "You folks from Southside sure ain't so friendly. I reckon you think you're too good for the likes of me."

"Not at all." Heather turned to Sir Edward. "You and Luther go on up. I'll come directly."

"Now you're talking." Bess winked at Heather.

"If you truly just want to sit here and talk," Heather pointed to the bench her companions had just vacated, "I'm happy to get better acquainted. I'd be curious to hear more about you, Bess. Your age? Where you grew up? Your family? What sort of schooling you've had—"

"Schooling?" Bess laughed as she sat back down. "You must be daft, Harry. Girls don't go to school in Westside. Even our boys don't get much schooling." She rolled her eyes. "My brother's lucky he can read—and no thanks to the school. 'Twas my dad who taught him." She lowered her voice. "And me too, although a lot of good it does me."

Heather frowned. "That's too bad."

"As for my family, my dad worked himself to death in the mines in Northside. That was a few years ago. But it was no surprise—most of 'em that works the mine don't live much past thirty. My older brother's there now. He's nearly twenty, but his days are numbered. And my mum makes her living, if you can call it that, making socks and whatnot."

"Your mum makes socks?" Heather tried to imagine this.

"Aye. She knits socks and mittens and scarves and such. She uses the finest wool, and they get sold over in your region—Southside. That's 'cause most folks in these parts can't afford such things." Bess rolled her eyes. "But the tariff the palace puts on my mum's socks makes it almost not worth the effort. They takes more'n half of her profits, they do." She lowered her voice. "That selfish old ogre. I hear he is sick. I know it's wrong, but sometimes I hopes he dies."

"You mean the king?" Heather tried not to appear alarmed by Bess's bold declaration.

"Aye. Our greedy king is taxing his people to death, he is. May not be so hard in your region, Harry, but 'round here, it's bad. Folks is lucky to afford their bread, they are." She looked longingly at the leftover food still on the table.

"You want that?" Heather pointed to the plates. She tried to appear nonchalant, but she was still absorbing what she'd just heard about the tariffs. Was it true?

"Don't mind if I do." Bess eagerly scooped all the leftovers onto one plate.

Heather considered Bess's words as she watched the hungry girl shove the food into her mouth, using the last crust of bread to wipe the plate clean.

"Thanks, Harry." Bess slid the empty pewter plate aside and smiled.

"You're most welcome." Heather smiled back, hoping she'd be able to gather more information. "You may be right about the tariffs being higher over here than in Southside. I've never heard much complaining over there."

"Of course not. They live too close to the palace to complain. Folks who complain get sent here. Or worse, they get sent to Northside. Working in Northside is nothing more than slavery, it is. Just ask my brother. Or my dad, God rest his soul."

"I didn't realize things were so bad." Heather sighed.

"I can tell just by looking and listening to you that you come from a soft sort of life." Bess got a dreamy look. "I reckon your folks are well off, aren't they, Harry?"

Heather shrugged.

"Sorry 'bout that." Bess frowned down at the table. "Didn't mean to get too fresh with you about your personal life. I knows better."

"It's all right." Heather studied Bess. She wasn't bad looking, in a common sort of way. Her auburn hair and green eyes were striking, but her fingernails were chipped and dirty, and the rouge on her lips and cheeks gave her a harsh appearance. But if she were cleaned up and dressed neatly, she probably would be pretty.

"Some folks say I'm too nosy." Bess wiped her mouth with the back of her hand. "But I likes talking to people. I likes hearing their stories. You know?"

"I do." Heather nodded. "Tell me, where did you get your fancy green gown? It matches your eyes." Bess's velvet gown, though frayed and dirty, once had been rather fine and probably quite costly. A gown that someone as persnickety as Princess Rose might have approved of when it was new.

Bess looked down at the stained bodice. "Came at a high price, it did." Her expression grew glum. "And I 'spect I'll be paying for it for the rest of my days. Speaking of such, if all you want to do is talk, I best be moving on." She looked hopeful. "I do likes you, Harry. You and me could have us a real good time." She leaned forward with interest.

"No, thank you, Bess. I meant what I said. I only wish to talk."

Bess sighed as she stood. "Thanks for the food, Harry. I gotta go." And before Heather could stop her with more questions, Bess moved on to another table—in fact, to where Michael and his friend were finishing up their meal. This made Heather curious. How would they react to Bess's advances?

Heather watched with veiled interest as Bess introduced herself using the same opening lines she had used on Heather and Sir Edward—as if she was warming them up.

"I'm happy to say I'm a visitor. I do not live in the Kingdom of Raspen." Michael's voice was loud enough for all to hear.

"Lucky man, you is." A stout fellow at a nearby table held up his ale mug. "'Ere's to you!"

"Aye," his companion agreed. "We've been talking about finding a new place to live—a place where we can afford to live."

Heather tried not to look too interested as she stood to leave, lingering as she fiddled with a bootstrap.

"Where I come from, folks like to say that the word Raspen is an acronym," Michael told them.

"What's your meaning?" the stout man asked with a creased brow.

"The letters in the word Raspen have a secret meaning. It's not about the common folks, but it's a description of the royal family." Michael grinned as he held his forefinger in the air. "The R in Raspen is for *rich*." He held up a second finger. "A is for *arrogant*, and S is for *selfish*." Several people laughed at this. "P is for *pride*, and E is for *entitlement*." Now he held up the thumb on his other hand. "And N is for *nincompoops*." Everyone burst into hilarious laughter.

Heather feigned an amused smile as she headed for the stairs. But if she were truly a man—and a commoner—she would go over there and poke that nincompoop's nose.

## Chapter Eight

Heather fumed as she went up the stairs to find the room at the end of the hall. What right had Michael, a foreigner, to judge her Kingdom like that? She paused in the hallway, listening to the rowdy talk and laughter down below. He was still entertaining the crowd at her father's expense.

But then she remembered how hungry poor Bess had been and how she'd gratefully eaten the scraps from their plates. Heather cringed at the memory of the discussion about the high tariffs, echoing the comments the others had made. How could that be true? It made no sense.

It was clear that Bess and her family were living in poverty. Yet she was a citizen of the Kingdom of Raspen, a monarchy Heather would soon rule. These discoveries were more than merely unsettling. They were disturbing. Did Heather's father fully grasp this reality? He had mentioned rearranging his council while she was gone, but would that truly remedy these troubles?

Sir Edward and Luther were making themselves beds on the wooden floor when she entered the small room. "What's this?" she asked. "What are you doing on the floor?"

"We saved the bed for you," Luther announced.

She frowned, remembering what Bess had said about the king's greed. "I feel selfish forcing you both to sleep on the floor. It's not right."

"You didn't really think we would share your bed?" Sir Edward looked shocked.

"No, no, of course not. But you two could share the bed and I could sleep on the floor."

"Nonsense." Sir Edward shook his head.

"Besides, it's not so different than sleeping outside under the stars." Luther sat on the floor and tugged off his boots. "Except there are no stars."

Heather chuckled, wondering what it really would feel like to sleep on a hard floor. She was willing to try but suspected it would make Sir Edward too uncomfortable.

"So you did not succumb to Bess's charms?" Sir Edward teased.

"I feel sorry for the girl." Heather told him a bit of Bess's pitiful tale. "And since her older brother is only nineteen, she must be my age or younger."

"It's a sad life indeed."

"I wish I could help her."

"How?"

"I don't know." Heather frowned. "But for now, I could give her a bit of money, if you think it would be all right."

Sir Edward shrugged.

"And later, when I'm queen, I could look into the reasons her family is so poor. She mentioned how they've suffered from unusually high tariffs."

He barely nodded. "I only recently heard about these

*unusually* high tariffs myself. And without consistency or reason. Unfortunately, we think this is the work of the councilmen your father probably has removed by now."

"Were Barnaby and Rupert lining their own pockets?"

"According to the records, there was good reason to suspect unfair collecting." Sir Edward let out a weary yawn. "There is some repair work to be done when we get back to the palace."

"But that doesn't help Bess right now. I feel so sorry for her. If I could just do something." Heather sighed. "I know it's a small thing, but I'd like to do it."

"That's generous of you, Princess Heather, but I'm afraid it will be just a drop in the bucket. Bess is one of many."

Heather held out her hand. "Yes, but her honesty has helped open my eyes. I'd like to thank her for it."

"Generosity is its own reward sometimes." Sir Edward sighed as he extracted a gold coin from the bag and handed it to her. "Be careful with how you present this to her. It could create problems."

She nodded. "I'll keep that in mind."

Her steps were lighter as she hurried down the stairs. She couldn't wait to see Bess's expression when she presented her with this unexpected gift. But when she got downstairs, she discovered Bess talking to a pair of rough-looking fellows who had just entered the inn. The men's words were coarse and unkind, and it saddened Heather to see Bess conversing with them. Because the men's backs were toward Heather, she was able to wave over their shoulders at Bess.

"Oh, Harry," Bess said happily, pushing past the men. "You came back."

"I wanted to speak to you," Heather said in her manly voice. "Alone."

Bess smiled happily. "Oh, I knew that you liked me, Harry."

"Come with—"

"Hold on there, boy!" The bigger of the two men rushed toward Heather, grabbing her by the arm and squeezing so tightly that Heather gasped. "What'd you think you're doing?"

"Talking to Bess," Heather said gruffly, twisting—and failing—to escape the man's steely grip.

"We were talking to Bess first," the other one growled, his round face red and puffy.

"Actually, I was talking to her first, and—"

"Shut your trap!" The man shook her so hard that her head snapped back and forth. She worried her hat might come off.

"But I'm just—"

"Who'd you think you are, taking Bess away like that, you nasty little runt?"

"Just a friend." Heather's voice trembled.

Holding a doubled fist in the air, the man put his grisly face close to hers. And just like that, he laughed, opened his fist, and pinched her cheek. "This boy don't even have whiskers." He turned to his friend. "And he thinks he's going to spend the evening with Bess?" Both men started laughing.

"Leave Harry alone," Bess snapped at them. "If he wants my company, he can have it."

"But we had you first," the other man shouted.

"Let me go," Heather commanded the man with the vise-grip. But instead of releasing her, he shook her hard once more, doubling his fist again and looking like he meant business. "I'll let you go, boy, after I teach you a lesson you won't forget."

Before he could hit her, someone jumped him from behind, pulling him off Heather. Fists flew, and Heather was thankful for the fencing and self-defense training her father had indulged her as a youth, often treating her like a son. But she really wished for a weapon to put an end to the mêlée.

To her surprise, Michael and his friend had come to her aid. But the thugs who picked the fight had backup too.

Heather spent most of her energy ducking and leaping to stay out of harm's way, but it wasn't long before the innkeeper got involved. Using a wooden stick to whack one of her attackers over the head, he soon brought the brawl to an end, and the two troublemakers were thrown out.

Before Heather had a chance to thank Michael and his friend, Bess ran up to her. "That was so brave of you, Harry." She batted her eyelashes again. "So heroic."

"I wanted to give you something." Heather slid the coin into Bess's hand.

"Ooh, my-my! Goodness gracious!" Bess's whole face lit up when she saw the coin's worth. "No one ever pays like this or up front—"

"It's *not* a payment. It's a gift. Use it to help yourself. And stay away from those men. If I come back this way again, I'll see if I can help you more."

Bess's eyebrows arched. "You mean it?"

Heather nodded. "Goodnight, Bess." As she hurried up the stairs, she wondered if Sir Edward had heard the ruckus below.

What would she tell him if he asked? Maybe some things truly were better left unsaid. She slipped into the room to discover Luther sleeping and Sir Edward's eyes half-closed as he attempted to read by lamplight. It was such a sweet, peaceful scene that she decided not to disturb them. She would keep the details of her downstairs brawling to herself. At least for the time being.

Just the same, she secured the latch on the wooden door, and when she knew Sir Edward was snoozing, she sneaked her sheath and dagger from the weapons bag and secured it to her belt before climbing into bed with her clothes on. No telling if those ruffians would come looking for her, but if they did, she wanted to be ready. In the meantime, she hoped to catch some shuteye. If the first day of her big adventure had been this wild—and they hadn't even crossed the monarchy's boundaries—she could hardly imagine the challenges the following days might bring.

As she attempted to settle in on the lumpy straw mattress that reeked of previous occupants, her mind was preoccupied by the image of a certain young man. Although her first impressions of Michael had been negative, the way he leaped to her defense impressed her. And, while it was unlikely and impractical, she wished she could get to know him better. But Michael and Sir Jonathan were headed to Southside tomorrow. And her party was to journey in the opposite direction. Really, what chance would she have of ever seeing him again? And even if she did, what difference would it make?

# Chapter Nine

Sir Edward seemed uneasy as they gathered their belongings in the early morning light. "Are you troubled about something?" Heather asked while Luther was preoccupied with his bedroll.

"I fear your generosity to that girl last night could create a problem this morning."

"What do you mean?"

He scowled as he gazed out the window. "See down there?"

Heather put her face close to the thick, grimy piece of glass and, peering down to the yard below, spied the figure of a woman. Moving from foot to foot as if to stay warm in the morning mist, her dark cape blew open, flashing her emerald skirt. "Oh, dear. I wonder what Bess is doing here so early."

"I suspect she's waiting for you."

"Whatever for?"

With a creased brow, Sir Edward tugged on his beard. "Why do you think, Harry?"

Heather grimaced. "Oh, dear."

Sir Edward glanced at his son as if he didn't want the boy to be privy to this conversation.

"I'll go down ahead of you two," Heather announced. "You can meet me at the stables in a bit."

"A good plan." Sir Edward nodded. "We'll purchase some food from the innkeeper. We can have our breakfast along the road."

Heather grabbed her bundle of clothes and hurried down the stairs. She was barely out the front door before Bess accosted her.

"Oh, I'm so glad you're still here, Harry."

"I—uh—yes. Good morning, Bess. Why are you here at this early hour?"

Bess reached into her woolen cape. "I brought you something."

Heather blinked in surprise as Bess held out a pair of knitted socks. "What?"

"From my mum. She was so happy about how you helped me last night, she insisted I bring 'em to you. They'll keep your feet warm while you travel."

Heather hated to take the socks. It probably was like taking bread from this impoverished family. But the look in Bess's eyes told her that to refuse would be an insult.

"Thank you, Bess." Heather reached for the socks. "Tell your mum thank you too."

"I won't trouble you anymore now." Bess backed off. "I knows you don't have time for the likes of—"

"Remember what I told you last night." Heather put a hand on her shoulder. "About helping you. When I pass this way again, I meant it, Bess."

Bess's eyes grew large.

"In the meantime, you need to see to yourself. I'm glad to hear you were with your mum last night. You should stay with her as much as you can. Perhaps she can teach you to knit or cook or sew." This probably sounded silly, Bess needed the protection of a mother.

"I'll do just as you say," Bess agreed. "I will await your return, Harry. God speed to you on your journey."

Heather touched the brim of her hat. "Until we meet again."

Bess waved and hurried away. Heather felt relieved as she went to the stable. Sir Edward had been wrong. He'd been worried that Bess was here to take advantage of Heather's generosity, not to gift her with a pair of thick, warm socks. As Heather tucked them into her clothing bundle, she was even more determined to help Bess and her family.

As queen, it would be a simple thing to lift them out of their deprivations. A word spoken by Queen Heather, and it would be done. But after hearing about the hardship of the mines, Heather was certain Bess's family wasn't the only one in need. A problem like this would require more than a one-word fix. Something bigger was amiss. With a kingdom as wealthy as Raspen, it seemed wrong—no, immoral—for anyone to be so impoverished. Somehow, Heather planned to put an end to it.

# Chapter Ten

As they journeyed through Westside, it grew clearer that the extreme poverty in Raspen was not limited to the likes of Bess and her family. Indeed, the farther they ventured, the more obvious it became that something terrible was wrong.

"Everything here looks so shabby and forlorn," Heather said as their horses plodded down a dirty Westside street. "So unlike what you see in Southside." She tipped her head toward a crumbling house with a collapsed thatched roof. And yet there was a raggedy old woman sitting on the doorstep as if she lived there.

Luther laughed.

"What is so funny?" she demanded.

"How many homes in Southside have you visited?"

Heather considered this. The boy had a point. "None that I can recall. But I've been inside plenty of shops, and sometimes I've even taken a peek into the house back behind. I know that some shops have had their problems, and I realize it's not always as perfect as it seems, but I have never seen anything that compares to this." She waved her hand toward a dilapidated cobbler's shop. The door was partially off its hinges, the paint was chipped, and behind a cracked window sat one pitiful pair of used women's shoes.

"Yes, well, the Southside shops must put on a show," Luther told her. "For the sake of prosperity."

"Put on a show?" Heather frowned at him. How much did he know?

"Certainly. How would it look if a Southside shop were to look impoverished?"

"Why should it be impoverished? Unless the shop is run by a lazy shopkeeper who drinks too much and can't get out of bed before noontime."

Luther glanced at his father. "Does she truly not understand?"

"Understand what?" Heather glared at him. Luther didn't usually speak to her with such blatant disrespect. But, to be fair, she didn't usually dress like a commoner either. Perhaps her masquerade had put her young friend too much at ease.

Sir Edward nodded, giving his son permission to speak candidly.

Luther looked curiously at her. "I suppose you do not know that the villagers in Southside are pressured to keep the appearance of prosperity for the sake of the kingdom."

She hated to admit as much, but this did ring a bell. "What are you saying?"

Luther shrugged. "As you know, Southside lies at the entrance of the palace. For that reason, all residents and shop owners are under a strict ordinance to maintain their properties with absolute tidiness."

"Yes, I'm aware there are laws about this. But it's for the sake of all the neighbors. It's not fair for one establishment to go to rack and ruin and drag down the others."

"That may be so. But some people who cannot afford to properly feed and clothe their families are forced to whitewash their walls and paint their window trim. They must neatly thatch their roofs and fill their window-boxes with colorful blooms. And not only must they sweep the walks clean each morning, but they must present themselves in a manner that suggests wealth and well-being. If they do not, they risk losing their properties and being relocated." Luther waved his hand toward a dingy little hut of a house. "To a place like this...or worse."

Heather gave Sir Edward a stunned expression. "Is that true? People are relocated like Luther described?"

He nodded.

"Penny for the poor?" a barefooted lad called out, stretching a dirty hand upward. "Or a piece of bread?"

Heather reached into her saddlebag, pulling out a hard roll that she had left from breakfast. "Here you go, boy."

He reminded her of a hungry sparrow as he snatched the roll from her hand, scrambling away to devour it before the other children spied him. But it was too late. One of the bigger boys landed on him, prying at least half of it away. And others, like hungry birds, flocked around them. Heedless of the horses' hooves, they jumped and cried out, begging for food. She tossed down an apple and, although Sir Edward and Luther followed her lead to share from their own supplies, they couldn't feed them all.

"We must hasten on our way," Sir Edward said, kneeing his horse into a trot. "Before we are mobbed."

Saddened and guilty, Heather kneed her own horse, and the three of them galloped away until their hungry entourage was out of sight. As they paused to regain their bearings, Heather felt sickened. "What is to become of these poor people?" she asked as she caught up with Sir Edward. Luther and the packhorse were a little way behind them, allowing her to speak more openly.

"That is, indeed, a good question." Sir Edward sighed.

"I never dreamed our subjects had it so hard. Why has my father allowed this?"

"You know King Reginald has been ill. The king has not traveled from the palace in six years or more. How can a king fix what he cannot see?"

"Why couldn't the people come to him? Why couldn't they present their case and get him to help them?"

"Truth be told, I'm not as well informed as I imagined. But I'm afraid the answer may lie with Rupert and Barnaby. I suspect they had gatekeepers." He shook his head. "I hate to admit it, but it is much worse than I expected."

"But how did it sink to this level? Six years is not so long. How could the kingdom have deteriorated in such a short amount of time?" Heather relaxed her reins, allowing her horse to keep pace with Sir Edward's. "I still do not understand."

"Over the years, your father has steadily surrendered his authority to the council."

"Rupert and Barnaby should be forced to live here. Along with any other councilman who ignores this kind of poverty." Heather stared at a row of shabby houses where raggedy children played with sticks and stones in the dirt. "And those children should be in school."

"I agree," Sir Edward said sadly. "But, alas, 'tis easier said than done."

This was true. Even with the crown secured upon her head, Heather would have difficulty crossing the Royal Council. Her father had complained often of their stubbornness and their inability to listen. But she had taken those comments in stride, determining that they were squabbling over unimportant trifles— not over the welfare of small children and whether they should be educated or housed or fed. "What am I going to do?" she said in quiet desperation, almost to herself.

"You are doing it *already*," Sir Edward assured her.

"What do you mean?" She turned to him. "Princess Rose accused me of selfishness for taking this pre-birthday adventure. I'm worried she may have been right. Seeing these people and their troubles, I feel bitterly selfish. I should not be seeking adventure. I should be back at the palace setting these calamities straight."

"Your adventure is opening your eyes, Princess Heather. That is the first step to remedying the problem. Surely you can see that."

She considered this. "Yes, you're right. But perhaps I should shorten our adventuring. After we visit Northside—and I can only imagine what we'll find there—we should hasten back to the palace. Then I can begin to deal with what needs to be done. And I am not speaking of a silly birthday party either."

"No, I thought not."

"That settles it. We shall go home a couple of days early."

"As you wish." Sir Edward looked relieved.

"It *is* what I wish. And it's the right thing to do." But the truth was that she was reluctant to cut her adventures short. They had barely begun. "But before we return, I want to spend at least one night in the Wilderness. Under the stars."

"So be it."

As they continued through the village, Heather tried to imagine what it would take to get these people back on their feet. Free handouts were only a temporary remedy to poverty, and people needed to help themselves. But if people were too downtrodden, it was hard to get back up. And, more disturbing than this, the palace was well off.

As she considered the things she took for granted within the walls of the palace, she felt ashamed. The golden chandeliers, richly woven tapestries, massive oil paintings, carved columns, marble floors…such opulence. And such a stark contrast to this poor little village. When she considered how much her sister might pay for a single gown sometimes only worn a time or two, she cringed. That money could feed ten households for a year. These realizations not only sickened her. They made her angry.

## Chapter Eleven

They reached the outskirts of Northside shortly before nightfall, making camp in a sweet-smelling field of wildflowers beneath a stand of tall oak trees. Luther built a small campfire, and together they worked to prepare a simple supper of beans with smoked venison, hard cheese, bread and jam, and jasmine tea.

Heather couldn't remember enjoying a meal more. After supper and a last cup of tea around the campfire, they took turns telling stories and stargazing. By the time Heather drifted off to sleep in the warmth of her bedroll, she had never felt more content, relaxed, and ready for sleep.

At first morning light, Luther started a new campfire, which they used to warm themselves as they prepared a breakfast of bacon, bread, jam, and tea. "It looks like another fine day," Heather proclaimed as she observed the clear blue sky. "Perfect traveling weather."

"And we may wish to spend most of the day traveling," Sir Edward told her as they broke camp. "From what I heard in Westside, Northside is best for just passing through. Not staying."

"I'm sure you're right. But I want to at least see it. With my own eyes."

As expected, Northside was far more troubling than Westside. Poverty and depravity ran rampant. Even the royal guards were a bit dodgy. Or perhaps they were disgruntled for being assigned to a difficult post. As they moved closer to the center of the village, Heather grew concerned. She wasn't a bit surprised when Sir Edward recommended they change course and travel along the outermost borders of the region, avoiding the inner crime-ridden streets altogether. "It's too dangerous," he told Heather as they rerouted themselves toward the outskirts. "A risk we can ill afford."

They had only gone a short ways before a small group of men rushed them from a side street. The first young man attempted to grab the reins of Luther's horse. Meanwhile, the other three ruffians brandished knives as if they were ready to slit a throat to steal a horse. Fortunately, these men were on foot. And thanks to Luther's quick thinking as he whipped his horse about, the young thug lost his footing and stumbled to the ground. In the meantime, Heather and Sir Edward drew their swords, taking the rest of the hoodlums by surprise.

"Off with you!" Heather growled, swinging her sword. "Before we call the guards!"

It wasn't long before the alarming event and the thugs were far behind them. In fact, the farther they got from town, the more it seemed like a merry lark. Heather and Luther laughed as they recounted the incident, exaggerating the dangers and relishing their brave escape. What a great story to tell when they got home. Imagine how shocked Rose would be to hear of it.

"I hate to interrupt your fun and games." Sir Edward pointed to his right with urgency as he turned his horse. "But I fear we must make a run for it."

As Luther followed his father, Heather glanced to see a group of horsemen approaching. There appeared to be six or seven, and because they were on horses, they could present a greater threat than the earlier villains. Indeed, they were close enough that Heather not only observed their menacing expressions but recognized some of the earlier thugs among them.

"I'm inclined to agree." Heather turned Zephyr about and, urging him to a fast gallop, she soon caught up with Luther. "Make haste!" she yelled. "And forget the packhorse. We can get by without him if need be."

The three of them galloped past the last of the village houses, heading into the agricultural countryside. As Heather kneed Zephyr into a full run, she felt thankful for these royal horses. No horse in the entire kingdom could match these steeds for speed. Even the packhorse managed to stay well ahead of the band of thieves.

Heather looked over her shoulder to see that the horsemen, although falling behind, were not giving up. She had no doubt they were robbers or worse. But their old nags could not match the king's horses for speed. Even so, Heather knew better than to let up on Zephyr. Leading the way, she had her eyes on the trees that bordered this meadow. She hoped they would find their refuge in the woods.

As exciting as this chase was—and nothing was better than flying across fields on the back of a swift horse—Heather's concerns grew. What if, despite their speed, they were unable to lose these thugs? As good as the royal horses were, eventually they would need rest, water, and care. What if this reckless band of lowlifes, eager to plunder, drove their horses on a relentless pursuit?

Although Heather, Luther, and Sir Edward were all experts with the sword, they were outnumbered. What if a battle ensued, and they were taken captive, or worse? Even if Heather confessed she was royalty—and even if the thugs believed her—it would not ensure her safety. With the kingdom in the shape it was in, she doubted there would be much sympathy for royal blood. Certainly not with these criminals.

Seeing a creek ahead, Heather slowed down long enough to instruct Sir Edward and Luther to go ahead of her into the water. "Travel upstream for a good ways. It will hide our hoof prints," she called as she turned her horse away from them. "I'll catch up to you later."

"Wait," Sir Edward said breathlessly. "You cannot—"

"No!" she insisted. "You do not question royalty. Do as I command."

Despite Sir Edward's cries of protest, Heather continued across the creek. Once she reached dry land, she ran Zephyr fast until she entered a brushy, overgrown area that would conceal horse tracks. Fully aware that she might run straight into the bandits, she turned Zephyr back around, galloping alongside the trail she'd just made. But this time she zigzagged right and left to make their path seem wider. To her relief, she reached the creek with no sign of the other horseman.

Turning Zephyr upstream, she paused behind a willow tree

for a moment. It seemed her backtracking, zigzagging plan had worked. She couldn't see any sign of the bandits. Yet she was certain she could hear the thundering of their hooves coming her way. Or maybe it was only her own heart pounding in her ears. Whatever the case, she kneed Zephyr, galloping through the creek until the waterway took a sharp turn. There she stopped, hiding in the shadow of a stand of oak trees. She tried to catch her breath as she waited, listening to the men's voices less than a quarter-mile away. She patted Zephyr's sweaty neck, loosened the reins, and allowed him to enjoy a small drink. She strained her ears, trying to discern their words as the men yelled to one another. But their voices quieted, and she thought her trick succeeded. The band had continued past the creek.

She urged Zephyr upstream, hoping and praying that her pursuers would ride into the brushy area then into the woods. This would allow her time to find Sir Edward and Luther and secure a safe place to camp for the night. As Zephyr moved quickly through the creek, she studied the banks along both sides, trying to determine where her friends had exited ahead of her. They'd had the good sense not to emerge onto the soft sand or mud areas, which would've left obvious tracks. Eventually, a rocky beach where the pebbles looked a bit uneven and dampened—as if horses had recently passed through—came into view. A wise choice. She could remedy the tracks.

She dismounted then led Zephyr to a grassy area. Grabbing a fallen branch, Heather returned to the beach to smooth out the telltale pebbles. She also took a few moments to splash water up and down the creek's edge so it didn't reveal a distinct path.

Satisfied that their trail was hidden, she hopped back onto Zephyr and continued into the woods.

Heather suspected the wild goose chase on which she'd taken the bandits had put more distance than she'd planned between her and her companions. She hoped to find signs of their path and track them, riding as long as Zephyr's strength held out. Even if she didn't find her friends tonight, it was prudent that she keep moving, to distance herself from the thieves.

The countryside grew even lovelier. As the oak trees gave way to evergreens, a beautiful, wild quality about this uncultivated land came into being. The thick forest floor, green and shady and cool, was abundant with ferns and lush vegetation. She knew from studying maps that this was the Borderlands. A terrain she'd heard tale of and longed to visit but had never been allowed to. It was too wild and dangerous. There were too many outlaws roaming freely. Bandits and villainous people from unfriendly kingdoms. No place for a princess. Yet she was here.

Unfortunately, it seemed some of the tales she'd heard were true. Pursued by murderous hoodlums and concerned for the welfare of her missing traveling companions, she was unable to fully enjoy the natural beauty.

As she rode through the woods, she told herself not to be worried for her friends. She felt certain that they, like she, would stay on the move. Sir Edward was full of wisdom, and Luther was smart. Even so, there was safety in numbers, and she longed to see their smiling faces again. But the farther she traveled, the less certain she was that she would meet up with them before sundown. It didn't help that poor Sir Edward would become sick with worry when the afternoon shadows lengthened. She hoped he would know not to double back to search for her. Surely he would recognize that she was being cautious. The last thing she wanted was for him to risk his and Luther's safety for her sake. But they would—because it was their job to do so and because they cared about her. God help them.

## Chapter Twelve

By midafternoon, Zephyr needed a rest and water. Heather was sure the bandits were a fair way behind. Seeing a shadow up ahead, she hoped the big triangular mountain forming it might provide her with a hiding place and perhaps a stream for refreshment. There, she would take a break and attempt to get her bearings. Unfortunately for her, Sir Edward and Luther had the map and compass as well as all the supplies on the packhorse and their gold. Not that she'd need gold out here in the middle of nowhere.

Although she'd been desperate for Harry's great adventure, this was not what she'd had in mind. Oh, she could imagine the stories she might tell one day. If she survived this.

"Of course you'll survive this," she said aloud to reassure herself as she rode. "You are Princess Heather the Indomitable." Wasn't that what she used to call herself during fencing lessons? Even as a young child, she'd acted fearless around Rose. Partly because Rose had seemed to fear almost anything outside the palace walls and partly because her father had encouraged her to take on new challenges. He had been grooming her for the throne for as long as she could remember. And he would not be happy to know that she was out in the Borderlands alone.

Riding toward the enormous dark monolith, Heather tried to remember her geography lessons. For a moment, she even closed her eyes, imagining the colorful map that hung above Sir Edward's sturdy oak desk. She recalled how he would point to spots and quiz Rose, Luther, and Heather about their names.

"Black Mountain," she said in wonder. "This must be it."

She knew this mountain was northwest of the palace—probably two or three days' worth of horse travel away. Not a comforting thought. Especially when she felt so eager to return home. More than anything, she wanted to tell Father all she had seen and heard—and not only about her adventure. She wanted him to know she wanted to help him, to see that vital changes were made. She was ready to partner with him in putting their kingdom back to order.

As she dismounted her horse at the foot of the mountain, she heard the sound of running water. To her delight, a narrow bubbling brook was only steps away. She led Zephyr to the water's edge. They both enjoyed a drink. Then she tethered him on a grassy bank and returned to explore what she thought might be the opening of a cave.

Although the forest around Black Mountain was dark and shady, she did not relish the idea of sleeping alone in the woods with bandits roaming about. But the safety of a cave—unless it was inhabited by beasts—appealed to her. If only she could find the opening again.

As she retraced her steps, she admitted there were worse spots to make camp. Not that she could make much of a camp. With no means to light a campfire and all the food, along with her warm bedroll, still on the packhorse—with Luther and Sir Edward— her camp would be sparse indeed. But a snug little cave might be beneficial.

To her pleasant surprise, she'd been right. There was a cave. Crouching down low, she crept through the short opening. She wished she had some source of light or flint to make a campfire. It was cool and damp, but come nightfall, it would provide welcome shelter. She squatted, listening intently, curious if anything else had made its home in here. But all was silent except for the nickering of her horse outside. About to go check Zephyr, she heard a noise within the cave. Cupping her ear with her hand, she listened to footsteps crunching on graveled rocks. The echo made it hard to determine the direction of the source.

Holding her breath, she remained frozen in this crouched position, afraid to make a sound as the steps drew closer. If it were a wild animal, it could be lethal to run. Instead, she slid her hand down her side, reached for her sheath, and opened it. She had just removed her dagger when she was jumped from behind.

Slashing her dagger toward her attacker, her arm was caught in midair with a hard smack. The dagger flew from her hand, clanging against a stone wall. This was man, not beast. As he pinned her to the rocky ground, she realized she was no match for his strength. Using the power in her legs, she pushed hard against his torso, flinging him from her onto the rock wall. She rolled onto her side, springing to her feet and about to bolt for the cave opening, when he leaped on her again.

They were rolling and flailing and wrestling on the loose rocks. If she could only grab a good-sized stone, she might be able to slam it into the thug's head and knock him out. But he did not let up, and before long, the wrestling match rolled the two of them toward the light of the cave's entrance.

Pinned again, Heather gasped for breath as she reached for a lethal stone. She raised it into the air just as the light from outside the cave illuminated her assailant's face.

"Michael!" she screamed.

"What?" Panting breathlessly as he straddled her, Michael peered down at her with widened eyes. "Harry?"

"Yes!" she gasped. "It's Harry. Get off me, you animal. Let me go this instant."

"I'll release you only if you promise to drop that stone—before you kill me."

She glared at him as the rock slipped from her grasp. "Me kill you? Isn't it the other way around?"

"I thought you were a bandit," he said as he climbed off her and crawled out of the cave's entrance.

"I thought *you* were a bandit," she said as she followed him out into the shadowy light of the forest. Still unsure as to whether he was trustworthy, she kept a safe distance, staring at him in disbelief and wishing her sword wasn't still on her horse.

"What is this?" Michael reached over and tugged on one of her braids. It must've come unpinned in the tussle.

"Nothing." She grabbed it from him, attempting to stuff it beneath her hat, only to discover her hat was gone.

"You're a girl!"

"You're a beast." She rubbed her bruised shoulder. "Why did you attack me like that?"

"Like I said, I thought you were a bandit." He held up his hands in a helpless gesture. "I'm truly sorry. If I'd had any idea it was you, I'd never have jumped you...*Harry*."

"Thank you so much," she retorted. "I'm going back to get my hat and my knife." She narrowed her eyes. "If you don't mind."

"Not at all." He grinned. "Perhaps you'd like some light. Rather dark in there, if you hadn't noticed."

She sighed in exasperation. "Thank you. A light would be most helpful."

He reached into his tunic and produced a candle stub, which he handed to her. Next, he pulled out a flint stone and proceeded to strike it to a flame. Using a stick, he lit the candle. "There you go, my lady."

Aggravated and relieved, she returned to the cave where, thanks to the candlelight, she located her silver dagger and her dusty hat, which she shoved onto her head. But instead of returning, she sat down and pondered this unexpected and undesirable turn of affairs. It made no difference that this young man had discovered she wasn't a boy. Really, why should he, a foreigner who made fun of her kingdom, give a hill of beans about the fact that she was masquerading as a boy? Why should she even be troubled? Except that it seemed to be just one more complication in an adventure which had become far too complicated.

# Chapter Thirteen

With her hat on and her braid tucked out of sight, Heather paused to regain some composure before she emerged from the cave and back into the light, walking with what she hoped would appear as dignity. Why she even cared was a bit of a mystery, but perhaps it was good practice for when she would rule as queen someday. Michael still waited, looking just as curious as he had been when she had left him.

"Thank you." She handed back the snuffed-out candle. "And if you will excuse me, I shall be on my way."

"Wait," he called out, following her to the brook.

"Leave me alone," she growled as she knelt next to Zephyr, dipping a hand in the stream's cold, rushing water.

"Not so fast." He stood above her.

"What difference does it make to you?" Kneeling on a flat stone, she bent down to wash her hands and face, cleaning off the dirt she'd picked up in their scuffle. She then removed her hat and proceeded to unpin her messy braids. She lined the hairpins on the rock then began to take out the braids to plait it again and pin it—much more securely this time.

Well aware he was watching her, she pretended to ignore him.

Using her fingers to comb and untangle her curls, she worked them into two tight braids and started re-pinning them to her head.

"Why are you pretending to be a boy?"

"None of your business."

He sat down on a larger stone a few feet away from her. "I beg to differ, my lady—"

"And quit calling me that. I am not your lady." She secured the first braid back in place.

"Your hair looks nicer down."

"Enough!" She growled with a hairpin between her teeth.

"Perhaps you are wondering why I should think it's my business, Harry." He grinned slyly at her.

"Perhaps I do not care. Nor do I believe you." She glowered at him as she began to secure the second braid. She knew she was doing a horrible job with it. Her handmaid would be scandalized at the unevenness, not to mention the dirt. She refused to think of what Rose would say.

Her only priority was to recreate the illusion that she was a boy and to do it quickly. What if the bandits happened upon them just now? It would be bad enough to be captured as a boy—but as a young woman? That was more than she cared to imagine.

"You may be interested to know that I have been in conversation with Sir Edward and Luther and—"

"What?" Her eyes grew wide as she gave him her full attention. "Is that true?"

He nodded. "I found them fleeing the bandits this morning. My friend and I got separated in our own attempt to avoid them.

When I came upon your friends, I guided them to what I hope is a safer route. Out of harm's way."

"Truly?" She blinked in disbelief.

"I swear to you, it's true. They told me how the three of you had been pursued by bandits and how you parted ways at the creek. You led the bandits away and commanded Sir Edward and his son to keep going." Michael scratched his head. "I find that interesting, Harry. You are a young woman, yet you are surprisingly brave. And you give your companions commands. And they take them."

"Yes, yes. But tell me more about my friends. They are safe? Both of them?"

"They were safe when I left them."

"And *where* did you leave them?"

He leaned over and smoothed the dirt between them, creating a map of sorts. "We are here, at Black Mountain—"

"I knew this was Black Mountain."

He smiled. "You're right. So we are here. And they are over there. And everything in here," he drew his finger through the dirt, "is crawling with bandits."

She nodded.

"I suggested Sir Edward search for you over here," he pointed to the other side of the circle he'd drawn for the mountain. "Meanwhile, I was to cross through the bandits and search for you in this area."

She smiled at him. "Thank you."

His brow creased. "But I'm unsure of what to do." He pointed to the bandit region again. "It's unsafe to take you back this way." He squinted at the sky. "And it's getting late."

"We probably have three hours of daylight left."

He pointed to his dirt map again, to the opposite side of Black Mountain. "This area here is called the Haunted Woods—"

"That's right. I remember."

"The bandits don't go there. Especially at night."

"Because it's haunted?"

He smiled. "They believe it is."

"But it's not?"

He shrugged. "Regardless, it may be the best answer. You will go around Black Mountain like this." He drew his finger around the circle in the dirt. "Until you come to the river."

"The Serpentine?"

"That's right. And you will stay there until I return for you." He ran his finger around the opposite side of the mountain. "With your friends."

She considered this. "No. Please, don't bring Sir Edward and Luther all the way back there." She ran her finger through the dirt, drawing a shortcut in the direction that would lead to Southside and the palace. "I want them to go home—as swiftly and cautiously as possible."

"Why?"

"I'm worried for their safety." She shook her head. "I never should've brought them on this perilous journey. I didn't realize how dangerous it would be. I want them to go home and speak to my father—" She stopped herself.

"The king?" Michael's earnest brown eyes were locked on her.

Ignoring him, she continued. "I want my friends to inform the proper authorities about the situation beyond the palace walls. Tell Sir Edward he must speak on my behalf and assure them that I am safe and that I will be home as soon as possible."

"In time for your birthday celebration"

She took in a fast breath. What was he saying?

"I know who you are, Princess Heather."

A sobering chill ran through her. With crooks and thieves as thick as fleas in these parts, it was dangerous enough to travel disguised as a commoner. But if her identity became known, it wouldn't just be her life at risk—it would be the entire kingdom.

# Chapter Fourteen

Heather was speechless. To deny his accusation would only prolong this uncomfortable conversation—and convince him he was right.

Michael's expression softened. "But I assure you that your secret is safe with me. As are you."

"Did Sir Edward tell you?"

"Not exactly." Michael ran his hands through his curly dark hair. "He insinuated you were valuable to the kingdom and that the king would appreciate your safe return."

Heather studied him, trying to assess his character. Was he an honest, well-meaning person eager to help? Or, more likely, was he a fortune seeker hoping for a potential reward? Perhaps it didn't matter. Sometimes the ends outweighed the means. The most important thing was to get home as soon as possible. "So, you know who I am. Can you help me get home?"

"I can accomplish that, Princess. Trust me."

"You will be recompensed generously for your time, I assure you."

"I'm not seeking payment of any kind." He sat up straighter.

"You seem to know much about me, but I know little about

you, Michael." She intensified her gaze. "Where are you from, and why have you come to our region?"

His lips curved into a smile. "The truth?"

"Why would I ask for anything less?" She locked eyes with him, reminding herself that she was soon to be queen, and just because he was charming, attractive, and well-spoken was no reason to lose her composure. Was it?

"I am from Mandela," he said solemnly.

"Mandela?" she echoed. "Our neighbors to the north?"

"That's right."

"My mother's family came from Mandela."

"Again, you are correct."

"But that still doesn't tell me why you are here."

"You shared your secret with me, Princess Heather, so I will share mine with you. But only because I come here in peace in the cause of diplomacy."

She frowned. "That sounds a bit foreboding. When someone speaks of peace in such a way, I hear the whisperings of war."

He nodded. "Because you are soon to be queen, and because you seem to be fair-minded and intelligent, I will speak frankly with you. The Raspen region that lies closest to our boundaries—Northside—has become a severe problem for Mandela."

"How so?"

He waved his hand behind him. "As you've witnessed firsthand, bandits, mayhem, and lawlessness abound in the North. And much of this anarchy has been seeping across our borders. Your citizens have rampaged and plundered our land, and our leaders are demanding retribution."

"War?"

"But not because of the gangs of unruly criminals. Your mines have steadily increased in size, slowly stretching northward, trespassing into regions that have been held by Mandela for centuries."

She grimaced. "I did not know this."

"My mission here in Raspen was to see the situation for myself and to speak to your father. My purpose was to get him to see reason and avert war. But when I reached Southside, I was informed of the King's infirmities and of the fact that his daughter, Princess Heather, was soon to be crowned queen. So I cut my visit short. As fate would have it, our paths crossed at the inn."

She shook her head in wonder. "That is rather amazing, don't you think?"

"It is serendipitous."

"Rest assured, Michael, I hear your concerns. If you will set Sir Edward and Luther on a homeward course then meet me as you have promised—"she pointed to the spot on the dirt map— "and help me to reach the palace safely, I will do everything within my power to set these troublesome problems in the north right. We will respect your borders. As queen, I can do this. As princess, I give you my promise that I will. But first I must get home."

"You too have my promise, Princess. After I see to your friends' safety, I will meet you as planned and tend to yours." As he looked into her eyes, something more than just a strong sense of reassurance came over her, along with an unexplainable rush of warmth.

"We are burning daylight." She stood, extending her hand

for a handshake. But as he touched her hand, the warm rush turned into pleasant tingles running all through her. What was happening here?

Still grasping her hand, he locked eyes with her. To her surprise, he pulled her toward him, wrapped one arm around her, and planted a kiss on her lips. She wanted to act affronted and perhaps even slap his face, but to her great consternation, she kissed him back. Then instantly regretted it. What had come over her? To her relief he looked almost as confused and surprised as she felt. Neither of them said a word as they backed away from each other.

"Well then." She pulled her hat back onto her head, securing it with pins, then moved toward Zephyr as she tried to get her bearings. "I will take that as the seal of our agreement." An embarrassed smile came over her as she slid into the saddle. "And I will hold you accountable to it."

He bowed. "I am delighted to be accountable to you, Princess."

Heather turned Zephyr and, nudging his sides with her heels, they headed across the brook. Despite the trials and fears of the day, her heart felt happy and light. Even the prospect of going into the Haunted Woods alone didn't dampen her spirits. At least she would be safe there. She hoped it wouldn't be long until Michael reunited her with her friends. Because Michael had given her his word. They would all meet again.

She traveled peacefully through the gloomy forest. Although Heather felt little concern about ghosts and goblins, she did grow a bit uneasy as the sky turned rosy. Darkness was not far off, and she had no desire to spend the night all alone in this place.

She wanted to urge Zephyr to pick up the pace, but her poor horse was tired. He was such a faithful steed, and she didn't want to push him beyond his ability. He lifted his head, and his ears perked. For a moment, she grew alarmed that bandits were afoot, and she prepared to draw her sword. But Zephyr's pace picked up without any urging from her. He had sensed water. It wasn't long until they were beside the river. She hopped off, allowing him to drink freely. She hoped it wouldn't be long before Michael showed up. She wondered if they would make camp or travel by night. Either prospect was fine with her.

She was adjusting a strap on Zephyr's bridle when the sound of a snapping twig caught her attention. Assuming it was Michael and her friends, she turned to see but was shocked to discover a strange man creeping up on her. He rushed toward her with a wicked look in his dark eyes. Her heart pounding, Heather grabbed her sword handle, but before it was out, she was seized from behind. The man was large, at least a foot taller than she. Strong as an ox, he easily pinned her arms behind her back, holding them tight.

"Release me at once," she growled as she attempted to kick him from behind. But it was futile. Her captor laughed in a deep voice, holding her so tightly she thought her arms were going to pop from their sockets.

"Got me a live one," the big man yelled. "Get your rope, Stefan. Help me with the little scrapper."

Unwilling to give up, she kicked and yelled, thrashing against the big man with all her might and hoping Michael was within hearing distance and about to come to her rescue. Meanwhile, the smaller man busied himself with binding her hands behind her back, tying them tightly with a rope as if he knew what he was doing. She let out one more yell.

# Chapter Fifteen

"Shut up, boy!" The big man backhanded Heather so hard that she fell backward. Before she could scramble to her feet, the smaller man bound them together.

"Hard to see much in this dim light." The big man was over by Zephyr now. "But feels like good horse flesh to me. Sweaty though. Been run hard. Nice saddle too. You steal this horse, boy?"

"That's *my* horse," Heather yelled at him.

"You a bandit?" the big man asked as he came back over.

"Most certainly not," she yelled, still hoping Michael might be near enough to hear her.

"What're you doing out here this time of night, boy?" Stefan asked. "You all alone?"

She could be mistaken, but she thought there was a hint of kindness in his voice. And for some unexplainable reason, she didn't think these two were part of the bandits from Northside.

"I lost my traveling companions," she said honestly. She started to explain that there were three of them traveling together but rethought this. "I'm traveling with a large group, and I wandered off. But I'm sure they must be nearby looking for me."

"Com'ere, Petre." Stefan grabbed the big man by the arm and, tugging him away, he spoke quietly to him.

Still sitting on the ground, Heather squirmed, trying to see if she might be able to escape her bonds. But they were so snug, her fingers were already getting numb. The only way out of this mess would be to use her wits.

"You should know that I'm here on the king's business," she called out, waiting to see if they were listening. "As are the men traveling with me." She waited for them to return and hoped she'd gotten their attention. "It won't be long before my friends send the Royal Guard out here looking for me. If they discover you've captured me and bound me like this, mark my words, it will mean prison for both of you. Or worse!"

"Shut up, boy!" Petre leaned down and picked her up, throwing her over his shoulder like a bag of grain. "Get the horse, Stefan."

"You'll be sorry," she yelled as he toted her off. "The king will punish you. I swear he—"

"Quit your bellowing," Petre yelled. "We ain't gonna hurt you none."

"If you shut your trap, it will go better for you," Stefan called from behind.

She did as she was told. Feeling the hopelessness of her situation, Heather allowed her limbs to go limp, focusing her energy on holding back frustrated tears as she tried to think of a way to escape her heartless kidnappers. How had she gotten herself into this? And where was Michael? More importantly, how was she going to get herself out of it? The third night of her big adventure, and here she was, trussed up like livestock and headed for certain disaster.

As she bounced atop Petre's rock-hard shoulder, a flickering sort of light danced among the trees. Unless she were imagining it, she could hear something that sounded faintly like music. She also smelled wood smoke and something like onions frying. When Petre deposited her to the ground, she landed on her backside with a hard thump and discovered she was in the midst of a Gypsy camp.

The merry music came to a stop as a group of colorfully dressed people began to gather round. Wearing bright silk scarves and gold jewelry, they peered down at her like she was an exhibit for their amusement.

"Are you Gypsies?" she asked.

Stefan rubbed his grisly chin with a creased brow. "We don't mind being called Gypsies so much, but we prefers to think of ourselves as *Travellers*."

She felt a rush of relief as she gazed about the faces. She quickly took in the brightly painted caravans, unusual clothes, printed scarves, and flashy jewelry. "I always wanted to meet a real gypsy—I mean traveller," she told Stefan.

Placing his hands on his hips, Petre bent down to peer at her. "Who *are* you, boy?"

"Harry." She gave him a cautious smile. "A friend of King Reginald. A king who is friend to the travellers."

"That used to be true." He frowned. "But, from what I hear nowadays, the king is a friend to nobody."

"But hasn't the king granted the travellers the freedom to roam through our land and to hunt our game? Is that not the gesture of friendship? Not all monarchs are as generous."

A heavyset woman with long gray hair and large golden hoops frowned down at Heather. "That was true enough, boy…once upon a time. But times change."

"Are you saying it's no longer true?" Heather narrowed her eyes. "As long as the travellers respect the laws of the king, the king will respect the travellers. I'm certain of it."

"*Humph!*" The woman turned to Petre. "What were you thinking, son? You went hunting for game but come back with *this*?" She smacked Petre in the back of the head. "Why did you bring us a boy? One more mouth to feed."

"We brought a horse too," Stefan called out as he tied Zephyr to a tree. Fortunately, he tied the rope loosely enough that Zephyr could munch on the tall grass growing nearby. He slapped Zephyr's flank. "A fine-looking horse too."

"The *king's* horse," Heather informed them. "I don't think you good people want to be caught with the king's horse in your possession. Not if you wish to remain in the king's good graces."

No one said a word for a long moment, and Heather hoped that she was getting through to them. "I've always heard that travellers were a friendly sort of people." She frowned. "Perhaps that was untrue."

"Why have you trussed the boy up like that?" the woman asked Petre. "He doesn't look big. Is he dangerous?"

"He was going for his sword," Stefan explained.

"Because I was being attacked from behind," Heather clarified.

"We saw bandits in the woods earlier," Petre told the woman. "We thought this fellow was one of them."

"I was being chased by bandits myself," Heather explained. "I thought Stefan and Petre were bandits too. I wanted to defend myself. But I never got the chance. They tied me up like a common criminal. For all I could tell, they were bandits."

"We tied 'em because he was kicking and yelling," Petre answered.

"How old are you, boy?" the woman demanded.

"Seventeen." Heather stuck out her chin.

"What are you doing out here by yourself?"

"I got separated from my traveling companions. I'm sure they're looking for me. It will not go well for you people if they find me here, bound and tied like an animal."

The woman glared at Petre. "There's enough trouble in this world without stirring up more."

"I know, Ma. But it was too dark to see much. The boy was going for his sword, and he may've been—"

"Untie him now," the woman commanded Stefan.

"Thank you, ma'am." Heather smiled up at her as Stefan pulled out a knife and cut Heather loose.

The woman pointed at Petre now. "And put the boy's weapons in a safe place."

Heather frowned in dismay. "But I need them for my—"

The woman shook her head. "You do not need them tonight."

Heather looked around the camp and nodded. "You are right,

ma'am. I'm sure I don't." Freed from her bonds, Heather got to her feet, brushing the dirt from her pants.

"I am Corina." The woman held out a hand.

"Pleasure to meet you, Corina." Heather gave her hand a hearty shake.

"Stefan and Petre are my sons." She slapped the big guy on the back. "Your woman is looking for you, Petre. Hurry before your dinner gets cold."

Corina turned toward the green and red wagon. "Adela. Your brother is back, and he's brought a friend. Bring them some food."

Heather walked over to Zephyr, where Stefan was still admiring him. "Mind if I remove his saddle?" she asked Stefan. "He's had a long day."

"Go ahead." Stefan watched as she bent down to loosen the cinch. "That's a good-looking saddle too. Bet it cost a lot."

"As I said." She stood to look him in the eye. "This is the king's horse. I am here on the king's business."

Heather had just set the saddle on the ground beneath the caravan when a dark-haired girl came down the steps. "Here's your supper, boy." She held out a bowl.

"Name's Harry." Heather grinned. "Thank you."

"I'm Adela." Her shy smile revealed a missing front tooth. "I'm sixteen years old. Ma said you're seventeen."

Heather nodded. "This smells good." She picked up the bent spoon and took a sample bite. "Tastes good too."

With her hand over her mouth, Adela giggled then hurried back to the caravan. Heather heard the girl talking to her mother.

She couldn't make out the words, but the tone in her voice was clear. Adela assumed that seventeen-year-old Harry was probably as interested in her as she was in him. Poor Adela—she would be in for a disappointment.

# Chapter Sixteen

As Heather ate the hot, spicy stew, she watched as people reconvened around the big, crackling campfire. Some of them still tossed furtive glances her way, whispering to each other as if trying to discern her intentions. Hoping to disarm them, she smiled and waved. Keeping a friendly distance might put them at ease.

She became less interesting to them as an elderly man pulled out his accordion and started to play. It wasn't long until someone called out, "Dimitrie, fetch your fiddle!" Before long, a young, dark-haired fellow tuned a violin and joined in. The tempo picked up, and soon other musicians playing tambourines and percussion instruments with gusto joined the group.

After her second bowl of stew, Heather went over to the fire, drawn as much to the lively music as the warmth. To her surprise, she was welcomed. The music was so energetic, she imitated the others by clapping her hands and tapping her toes. This whole scene of musicians playing, people dancing, and orange sparks racing up into the blackened sky was enchanting.

Heather couldn't help but watch the young fiddler. Not only was Dimitrie a wonder on his violin, but he was strikingly handsome too. What a delight it would be to dance around the campfire with such a romantic figure. Of course, that could never happen while she was disguised as Harry. But this music did entice one to dance. As if reading her mind, Adela grabbed Heather by the hand, and they danced around the fire with the others.

Heather felt a bit awkward and uncertain at first. These fast steps were new to her and unlike the ballroom dances she'd learned as a girl, and she wasn't used to taking the lead. But she quickly discovered such conventions made no difference here. These people danced from their hearts, and no one seemed to mind if you stepped on a toe or two.

The merrymaking went on for a good while, but as the moon dipped into the treetops, the crowd began to thin. Children and old people called out sleepy goodnights, and eventually just a handful of younger people hovered around the fire pit, which had burned down to a small pile of red coals. Dimitrie was the only musician remaining. He played a soulful song that was so stirring, Heather almost wanted to weep.

Once again, she remembered Sir Edward and Luther. She hoped they were not too worried about her and that they were resting well. Despite this evening not turning out as she had planned, it was a relief to know that Michael had encouraged them to go home. At least she hoped he had. But was it possible he had hoodwinked her? Her cheeks grew hot as she remembered that kiss. Had she fallen for a trick? What if he were on his way to his own kingdom, encouraging them to launch an attack on Raspen? It was all too much to mull over, and she was too tired to think clearly anyway.

Heather didn't even try to hide a big yawn, partly because she was exhausted and partly because she was concerned about Adela's attentions. The girl had stayed faithfully by her side for most of the evening. Even now, she was standing uncomfortably close to Heather.

"Dimitrie is a good musician," Heather said quietly.

"Aye. He is." Adela nodded.

"Not too bad looking either." Heather winked at Adela.

Adela glanced over at Dimitrie. "Aye."

Keeping her voice low, Heather continued, "And if I'm not mistaken, I think he's had his eye on you tonight." This was true, but Heather knew she might be playing it up too much.

Adela turned to her in surprise. "Me?"

Heather nudged her with an elbow. "Well, you could do worse, eh?"

Suddenly, Adela studied Dimitrie, almost as if Heather had hit a nerve. Why shouldn't Adela be swept away by the young man's good looks and musical ability? Really, the fellow was dreamy. She couldn't tell if he had any genuine interest in Adela, but perhaps that would change.

Heather yawned again, this time stretching her arms out the way she'd noticed some of the fellows doing. "I'm going to call it a night. But I'll understand if you want to stay and listen to Dimitrie play some more."

"Aye, that's just what I plan to do." Adela's eyes were fixed on Dimitrie now.

Satisfied that Adela would soon forget all about "Harry," Heather said her goodnights and slipped away. First, she checked on Zephyr, and for a moment she even considered saddling him up and making a quiet getaway. But she didn't see her saddle nearby. She hoped Stefan hadn't appropriated it. Plus, she knew her weapons were stashed "safely" away. Perhaps the wise choice would be to make her departure by daylight.

Thankful she was wearing the warm woolen socks Bess had given her, Heather kept her boots on. Layering on her extra clothes and woolen cape for warmth, she proceeded to make a bed in some loose straw beneath the caravan. As she nestled into her surprisingly comfortable nest bed, she was felt certain no one would attempt to stop her in the morning and hoped they would take her warning about stealing the king's horse seriously and return her saddle and weapons to her.

Pulling her cape more snugly around her shoulders, she decided that being kidnapped by gypsies (or travellers) had been a blessing in disguise. Not only did she get an amazing once-in-lifetime experience and some interesting food, but she didn't need to worry about being captured by bandits, and she would probably enjoy a good night's sleep.

She smiled to think what Rose would say if she could see her sister. It would certainly be a scathing scolding. She tried to imagine Rose in a similar situation, but all she could see was her sister with her nose turned upward, refusing to eat their food or to mix with such undesirable people. Might do her some good if she did.

Although she was relieved to be a guest in the travellers' camp and not a captive of bandits, there was a small fly in the ointment. The missing Michael. She had convinced herself that she had not been tricked. She had always been a fairly good judge of character, and she believed Michael's to be good.

As she closed her eyes, she prayed that nothing had gone wrong for him on his way to find Sir Edward and Luther. He seemed a savvy warrior—their wrestling match in the cave had proven that. She hoped she would meet up with him tomorrow. Her plan was to continue to take the route he had drawn out for her on the dirt map. Surely they would cross paths again.

Heather had barely slipped into a slumber when she awoke in a state of alarm and anxiety. With a rapidly pounding heart, she wondered if it was a nightmare—and then she realized her mouth was covered by something that made it difficult to breathe. In the same instant, she was dragged from her spot beneath the caravan. She tried to kick and scream, but the large hand crushing down on her lips made noise impossible—and now there was another pair of hands holding her legs.

All the lanterns were out in the camp, making it too dark to see faces as the nefarious duo toted her away like a large stick of firewood. Was this Petre and Stefan? And if so, why would they do this? Did they think she had money? More likely, it was her mention of the king. She probably had enticed them to seek ransom.

As she was transported away from the gypsy camp, her mind raced like a startled herd of wild ponies. Why would Petre and Stefan, who had acted like her good friends around the campfire, treat her in such a fashion? And what would Corina say about this? Or even Adela?

Or perhaps Heather had been foolish to trust these people at all. Sure, gypsies knew how to have a good time, but they also had reputations for kidnapping, stealing, and trickery. Why hadn't she simply abandoned her saddle and weapons and slipped away on Zephyr when she'd had the chance? Oh why, oh why, had she been such a fool?

After she'd been carried for a fair distance—surely out of hearing range of the slumbering camp—she was gagged with a rag tied tightly over her mouth, and something that felt and smelled like a burlap bag was thrown over her head. Once again, her hands and feet were bound. But overhearing her captors exchanging a few words, she realized these were not the gypsy brothers. And it was not a comforting thought.

She was hoisted upward then she was slung like a sack of cornmeal over the back of a horse and secured into place. And off they went into the night.

As she bounced along on the horse's back, a tiny sense of relief that the abduction was not the handiwork of her gypsy friends came over her. It had hurt to think the people she'd eaten and danced with had betrayed her.

However, if this wasn't the gypsies' doing, the only logical explanation was that she had fallen into the hands of bandits. Where were they taking her? And, more concerning, why? She could understand them wanting to steal her horse and belongings, but why would they want to kidnap a boy?

More importantly, how was she going to get away from these diabolical hooligans? Men with the gall to sneak into a gypsy camp in the middle of the night. Somehow she had to escape them. And she had to get back to the palace. Even if she had to do it alone, she had to go home.

During the bumpy ride that was giving her rib cage a beating, Heather knew, perhaps better than ever before, that Raspen was in grave danger. More than ever, her father's monarchy needed a strong and fair leader—someone brave enough to make some important changes—not a willful, foolish, adventure-seeking young woman who was helpless and hogtied onto the back of a horse. What if she couldn't get out of this? What if, instead of Queen Heather, the kingdom fell into the hands of Queen Rose?

Despite Rose's shortcomings—and they were numerous— Heather loved her sister. At the same time, Rose would never be up to the task of ruling the kingdom. Not in the way the kingdom deserved to be ruled. If anything, Rose would continue right along the path that the crooked counselors had taken. Collecting tariffs with no regard for the well-being and welfare of the people, turning a deaf ear to reports of crime running rampant. It would be no surprise if surrounding kingdoms launched a war against Raspen unlike anything these regions had ever seen.

Yet, as badly as Rose longed to be queen, she had no inkling of what she was up against. With her focus on riches and luxurious living, combined with her reluctance to step outside the palace walls, she had no idea what was coming her way. Heather could imagine her selfish, naïve sister bedecked and bejeweled, thinking she was ready for her new role of *Queen Rose*, while neighboring kingdoms would be equipping their troops and preparing to attack.

As these grim revelations settled upon her like a great black cloud of doom, Heather realized that Rose had been correct about one thing. Rose had accused Heather of selfishness for taking her little escapade. Although loath to admit it, Heather could not deny her sister had been right.

## Chapter Seventeen

The loose weave of the rough burlap bag allowed small squares of light to penetrate, showing Heather that, after what seemed an endless night, dawn had broken. But still they did not stop moving. She wondered how long she'd been slung across the back of this horse…four, five, maybe six hours? How far had they gone, and in which direction had they traveled?

Eventually the horse came to a stop, and, to her relief, her less-than-comfortable journey seemed to be over. Someone was getting her down.

"Can you stand, boy?" a male voice asked as the speaker set her on her feet.

Although she wasn't sure how steady she felt, Heather mumbled, "Yes," struggling to balance with her feet still bound together. She had to get her bearings, to inventory the situation, and somehow use her wits to find an escape.

As the bag was removed from her head, Heather was surprised that her hat, which she'd pinned into her braids yesterday, was still in place and that the lanky man before her did not look like a dangerous bandit. Fair-haired and tall, he looked to be about her father's age but in good health. Dressed in respectable clothing, he had a sword at his side, and could have passed for one of her father's knights, although she didn't know him. His somber expression was impossible to read. He probably would be good at card games.

"I will relieve you of the gag, boy, if you promise to keep quiet," he said in a civilized tone.

She nodded. A dozen questions raced through her mind. Who were they? Why had they kidnapped her? And the most troubling question: Where was Michael? But she was determined to keep her promise by keeping her mouth shut. At least for the time being.

"You thirsty, boy?" the other man called out. She glanced over to see that this man was shorter and rounder than the first one. He was tending to the horses, and to her surprise, there was Zephyr happily grazing with the other three alongside a fast-moving section of river. And he was saddled—with her saddle. These men must've spotted it when they nabbed her horse.

"You hear me, boy?" the short man demanded. "Are you thirsty? Hungry?"

"Yes," she said in a raspy voice.

"I'll untie your hands and feet," the first man told her, "if you give me your word that you won't run."

"I won't run," she assured him, knowing full well that she'd spoken a bald-faced lie. She would take off the first chance she got. But not right away. She needed to gain some trust from her captors first. And to wait for the right moment. But that would give her time to create a plan.

Freed from her bonds, Heather wobbled over to accept the

tin cup of water that the short man offered her. She drank every drop, waited as he filled it with more, then emptied it again. With her thirst satisfied, she sat by the campfire that the taller man was starting to build.

Rubbing the feeling and warmth back into her fingers and toes, she pretended not to eavesdrop as the men conversed. As she listened, she concluded that the taller man's name was Garret and the shorter one, who was working on their meal, was Martin. Somehow, although she had no solid proof of this, she began to suspect that these men were connected to Michael. Maybe it was their manner of speech or the way they seemed to be on some sort of mission. But something about these two men did not sit right with her. Michael must've told them she had value as a royal hostage.

How else would they have known her whereabouts? It was a bold move to sneak into the gypsy camp and steal her away like that. And more than a little disturbing. The idea that Michael might have tricked her with his sweet talk—that he might be using her for his own personal gain—cut to the core.

"You sure this is the right spot?" Martin asked as he arranged a metal tripod pot-stand over the fire.

"It's exactly as described," Garret told him. "The bear rock by the river. Remember?"

"Shouldn't they have been here by now?" Martin hung a pot of water on the stand.

"No telling."

As she listened, her mind was fast at work—leaping from side to side like a fencing match. She knew better than to jump to conclusions. Sir Edward had taught her this from an early age. Perhaps she was wrong to assume these men were associated with Michael or that Michael had betrayed her.

Yet she felt certain these fellows weren't part of the bandits' group and equally certain they were not citizens of Raspen. That posed the question: Why were they here? Was it possible they were from Mandela, like Michael? But even if they were, it did not mean they were friends of Michael's. She had no proof of that.

Heather had been taught to discern a person's character—a skill that Sir Edward had encouraged her to develop and use. She knew how to study a person, the way his eyes moved, the number of words he used, the way he used his hands, all could help determine a man's sincerity. Of course, this reminded her, once again, that she had believed Michael to be genuine. She really wanted to continue believing that. But was that foolishness?

So much was at stake. She had to be wise and figure this out. Who were these men? Where were they from? Where were they taking her? And why? Of course, those were not questions she dared ask. But perhaps she could soften them up a bit by starting with a less intrusive inquiry.

"Are we in the Wilderness?" she asked, mindful to keep her voice pitched low.

Martin gave her a curious glance then turned to Garret, as if he were unsure how to answer.

"I just wondered," she continued. "I've never been to the Wilderness before, but I always wanted to see it."

"Well, you're right," Garret informed her. "This is the Wilderness."

She nodded. "I thought it looked different than the Borderlands."

Martin handed her a bowl of porridge and a chunk of yellow cheese. "Slim pickings today. Seeing as we didn't have a chance to catch any game or fish."

"Thank you," she said gruffly.

No one spoke as they ate their meager meal, but both men were looking anxiously over their shoulders, almost like clockwork, keeping an eye out for whomever they hoped to meet. Was it Michael? And if it was, what would she do? What could she do?

"You are not citizens of Raspen, are you?" She tried to continue with nonchalance as she handed her empty bowl back to Martin. "I noticed a different accent."

Martin frowned at Garret as if seeking direction again. But this time Garret shook his head. So much for gathering information.

Garret's reluctance to be forthcoming felt like its own answer. Of course, they were up to no good. Why else would they sneak into a gypsy camp and cart her off in the middle of the night? But what sort of wickedness did they have up their sleeves? If they knew she were royalty, which seemed highly unlikely unless they were connected to Michael, she would assume they planned to hold her for ransom. Or perhaps some kind of political gain. They were awaiting someone. Was it someone who would pay them off? And if that were the case, she and Raspen were in serious trouble.

It was time to get away from them—or at least try. She was about to tell them she needed to go relieve herself in the woods when Martin stood. Cupping a hand to his ear, he looked toward the woods.

"Horse's hooves," Martin announced. "Not far off."

"That's probably them." Garret grasped his sword. "But just in case, be prepared."

Martin reached for his own sword.

Heather knew this was her only chance—a meager one, indeed, but one she could not afford to miss. Seeing the men focused on whatever was coming through the woods, she glanced to where Zephyr was still tied by the river, saddled and ready to ride. Spying a path of dewy grass between her and the horses, she hoped it might muffle the sound of her footsteps.

Holding her breath, she kept her eyes fixed on the men's backs and slowly stood, backing away from the campfire then slipping as quickly as she dared toward the horses.

With no time to look back and with her heart pounding in her ears, she untethered all four horses, hoping the others would be spooked and run off, allowing her more time to get away. In one swift motion, she flew into the saddle and dug her heels into Zephyr's sides. Her faithful steed took off like an arrow shot from a crossbow, and Heather leaned into his neck, urging him to run full speed. She would be followed.

As Zephyr galloped along the sandy riverbank, her eyes remained fixed on the river, watching for a shallow place to cross or perhaps a calm section where Zephyr might swim.

She heard the men's voices calling out from behind her and knew that her abductors were fast on her trail. She tugged the reins, urging Zephyr directly into the chilly river. As soon as his hooves hit water, she realized it was flowing faster than the surface revealed. And just as quickly, she knew they were in trouble.

Zephyr neighed as he struggled to keep his head above the fast-moving water.

His only chance was for her to dismount. Sliding off the saddle, she slipped down his rump and, neck deep in the icy water, held onto his tail as she urged him onward. "Go, Zephyr!" she cried out. "Swim to the other side!"

Halfway across the river, despite her best efforts to hold on, she was jerked down by a massive undertow, and Zephyr's tail slipped from her grasp. Sucked down beneath the rumbling water and unable to breathe, she felt herself being pummeled and tumbled by its powerful current, rolled about like a helpless rag doll. Her lungs burned for air as she clawed and kicked against the water's domination. Determined not to give up, she used every bit of strength to fight her way back to the surface. Her goal was to extract herself from the powerful pull of the river, but it would not surrender its hold. And then something inexplicable happened. It all slowed down. Suddenly Heather was encompassed with a wonderful sense of peace and well-being. She entered a warm, golden world filled with goodness and light and love. There, up ahead, was her father. With a huge smile on his beaming face, he ran toward her, his arms outstretched wide and welcoming.

# Chapter Eighteen

Sir Edward had felt Michael was trustworthy from the first time they'd met in the inn. The young man seemed intelligent, upstanding, and sincere. And Sir Edward had always been a good judge of character. Or at least he liked to think so. As a result, he couldn't have been more pleased than to run into the young man again—right when they'd needed assistance—wandering out in the Borderlands and failing to reconnect with Princess Heather.

"Pure providence," he said to Luther the following day. "A happy twist of fate." The sun was just dipping low into the sky as the pair of them reached the outskirts of Westside. Allowing their horses to slow down after a full day of travel, they used this time to converse.

"Running into Michael and Sir Jonathan?" Luther asked.

"That's correct." Sir Edward let out a weary sigh. "Because as much as I wish I were a spry young man fit to race from bandits and rescue our princess day after day, I'm relieved that our princess has commanded otherwise. And I'm glad she had the good sense to strike an agreement with Michael to escort her back to the palace."

"And you feel certain Michael will get her back safely? You truly believe him to be trustworthy?"

"I do." Sir Edward was tempted to tell Luther all that he knew, but he had promised to protect Michael's secret. "I have reason to believe Michael is as anxious to return the princess safely to her father as we are."

"I hope you're right."

"Michael is traveling with able-bodied men, Luther. Fit to defend and protect our princess to a greater degree than you or I could do." Sir Edward frowned. "If I had known the adversaries out there were as bad as they are, I never would've agreed to this trip."

"But it was fun." Luther grinned. "I have some great stories to tell my friends."

"And some stories that cannot be repeated," Sir Edward reminded his son.

"Where do you think they are right now?" Luther peered toward the west.

"According to the route Michael showed me on the map, cutting diagonally through the Borderlands, their party should reach Southside ahead of us." Sir Edward looked up at the darkening sky. "He's traveling with spare horses, which allows them to move at a good pace. Plus, the moon will be nearly full tonight. Good for traveling."

"Perhaps we should continue our journey too," Luther suggested.

"No," Sir Edward declared. "We will stop at the inn for the

night. Rest our horses and get a good night's rest. Be ready to leave at daybreak."

As Luther tended to the horses, settling them in the stable, Sir Edward headed for the inn. So much had transpired these past few days, he found it difficult to believe that it had only been four nights since they had stayed here. And while the accommodations had seemed rather meager and squalid at the time, he looked forward to these amenities tonight. However, he was dismayed as he entered the loud, crowded room. What if they were full?

"Have you a room?" he inquired of the innkeeper.

"I do for you." The round-faced man grinned eagerly. "But only if you pay like you did last time. Otherwise, we are full. Already people are paying to sleep on the floor."

Sir Edward reached into his pocket, extracting the single gold coin he had put there for this purpose. The rest of their traveling funds were still secure in his money belt, not far from his dagger. "One room, please."

The innkeeper frowned. "Only one room? I can give you two—for two of those." He eyed the coin greedily.

"It is only my young son and myself. One room is sufficient. Thank you."

The innkeeper looked disappointed but accepted the coin, calling over a woman who was setting several large mugs of ale in front of some diners. "Tell them fellows at the table by the door that they'll be sleeping on the floor tonight," he said.

The woman glared at him. "You 'spect me to give them bad tidings, do you?"

"Just say someone made a mistake," he growled, "else you'll be sleeping on the floor too, woman."

She said something unladylike then marched over to break the news.

"I'm surprised you're so crowded," Sir Edward told the innkeeper, "in the middle of the week too."

"Did you not hear the news?"

"What news?"

"That the king is dead."

Sir Edward let out a gasp and clutched his chest. "King Reginald is dead?"

"Aye. Died in his sleep last night, he did."

Sir Edward tried to regain his composure, but a hard lump was growing in his throat. "You know this for certain?"

"Aye, it's been the talk o' the town all day. And the palace ain't wasting no time neither—the king's funeral is tomorrow." He jerked his thumb toward the crowded inn. "That's why everyone's traveling just now. They all wants to see the funeral. And they all wants to see the queen getting crowned. And then there's the queen's eighteenth birthday. Three big events all in the same week. It's a holiday."

"Do you know what time the king's funeral will be?"

"In the afternoon, I heard."

"I'd like two suppers," Sir Edward told him. "And we need food for the road. We will depart early. Before daybreak." He removed a second, less valuable coin from his coat, but a generous one just the same, and handed it to the innkeeper. "As promptly as possible, please."

"You got it."

As Luther trudged into the inn, Sir Edward could tell that he too had heard the news. He hurried to his son, putting an arm around his shoulders. "At least he died in his sleep," he said.

"The men in the stable were celebrating," Luther confided. "As if our king's death were a good thing."

"Some people have no respect."

"It just seems wrong." Luther nodded toward the door. "Bess is waiting outside. She asked to speak to you."

"Bess?" Sir Edward frowned.

"Remember that woman that Princess Heath—" Luther stopped himself. "The one Harry helped last time we were here?"

"Why does she wish to speak to me?"

"She said it's in regard to, uh, Harry. I didn't even recognize her, Father. She's not wearing those fancy clothes."

Sir Edward pointed to a table with a couple of empty stools. "Sit there, son. Our supper is on its way. And then we'll retire early. We will sleep a few hours, just long enough to refresh ourselves, and then we'll travel by the light of the moon as fast as we can go. It's the only way to ensure we reach the palace in time for King Reginald's funeral." He sighed. "I only hope that our princess is nearly there by now."

Sir Edward's steps were heavy as he went outside. He glanced about the yard until he spotted a lone woman standing by a tree. Dressed in plain clothing, she didn't look much like the painted girl from the other night. He hurried toward her, curious as to why she wished his audience.

"Thank you for speaking to me, sir." She gave a little curtsy. "I spotted you and your son on the road, so I hurried over here in the hopes that Harry may be with you. I would've asked your boy, but I worried it may not be proper."

"I appreciate that." He frowned.

"Please, tell me, where is Harry?"

"Harry has taken another route. He should be reaching Southside before us."

"Oh." She let out a relieved sigh. "So, he has come to no harm then?"

"No," he reassured her. "Harry should be just fine. Although, like us, he will be disturbed to hear of the king's demise."

"Aye." She nodded sadly. "I know Harry was quite fond of the king. I wish I'd not spoken ill of him like I done. If you see Harry, please, tell him I'm sorry." She curtsied again. "Thank you, sir." She hurried off into the shadows.

Sir Edward scratched his head as he went back into the inn. Was it possible that Princess Heather's kindness had generated such a remarkable transformation in that young woman? Or, more likely, was poor Bess smitten with young *Harry*? Whatever the situation, Sir Edward felt glad for Bess. Maybe she had reached a turning point. He could only hope.

As Sir Edward and Luther prepared for bed, few words were spoken. Sir Edward suspected his son's heart was nearly as heavy as his own. Despite the years of the king's steady decline in health, they had both enjoyed his company, his generosity, his wit, his spirit. And now he was gone. Sir Edward hated to think of how Princess Heather would receive this sad news.

Knowing the sensitive heart of the princess as well as her

devotion and love for her father, she would feel guilty for not having been by his side. She might even blame herself for his death, assuming that he had been worried for her welfare. And to be sure, if King Reginald had nurtured any idea or inclination of what was going on in his neglected kingdom, he would indeed have had cause for concern. Fortunately, the king had most likely died without knowing. And Sir Edward hoped that meant the king had died peacefully. That was worth a lot.

# Chapter Nineteen

The road to Southside, illuminated by moonlight, was busy with travelers in the wee hours of the morning. Some moved slowly on foot, others piled into the backs of wagons, and a fortunate few, like Sir Edward and Luther, passed more quickly on horseback. But all seemed intent on getting to the palace in time for the king's funeral.

"Being out here like this feels like a dream," Luther said. "But not a happy one."

"There is something to be said for traveling by moonlight," Sir Edward admitted. "But I agree. 'Tis not a joyous journey."

"Do you think Princess Heather knows yet? That her father has died?"

"Bad news travels faster than a wildfire. If our princess has not yet reached Southside, I'm sure she has crossed paths with someone who has informed her."

"I feel sorry for her." Luther looked earnestly at Sir Edward. "I cannot imagine how I would feel to lose my father."

Sir Edward sat straighter in the saddle. "Fortunately, I am in good health, my son. I expect to be around for many more years."

"For that I am thankful." Luther sadly smiled. "But I still feel sorry for Princess Heather."

It was midmorning when they reached the outskirts of Southside. To Sir Edward's surprise, a feeling of festivity tingled through the air. As if the villagers were preparing for a celebration instead of a funeral. Was this representative of how much they resented their king?

As he and Luther stopped for water, both for themselves and their horses, he overheard snippets of conversation from the locals. The consensus seemed clear—no one was concerned over the king's demise. And all were quite optimistic over the prospects of Queen Heather's rule.

"She's a good one, that Princess Heather," the cobbler told them. "Stops by my shop and gives me business just as if she were one of us. Commissioned a fine pair of boots just a month ago. To give to some young boy, she told me."

"Kind, she is," a mother with a toddler in her arms said. "Saw me in need one time and helped me out."

"And she always waves and says hello as she passes," an elderly man added. "And she calls me by name, she does."

"Aye. And when she rides through the village, she is not dressed in finery like that other snooty sister," a young woman said. "Princess Heather has a heart, she does. I can tell by looking into those blue eyes."

"I know she will be a fair ruler," the old man said. "Just like her grandfather was fair. And even King Reginald, back before he lost his wife and fell ill. God bless the king," he said reverently.

"And God bless the new queen!" the young woman exclaimed.

"It will be a new day for Raspen," an old woman said. "A new day, indeed."

Sir Edward felt encouraged as they continued through the village. The people were right. With Heather as queen, they would be in good hands. However, he knew it would not be a smooth or easy journey. And despite his general dislike of politics and his frequent refusals to join the Royal Council, it was time to change his thinking. After seeing what little they'd seen of the sad dysfunction in the kingdom, he was ready to stand beside Queen Heather and accept her invitation to step into leadership as Head of the Royal Council. No question about it.

"See to the horses," he instructed Luther as they came to the Royal Stables. "When you are done, go home and dress for the funeral procession. Tell your mother I will be delayed. I must discover whether our princess has arrived yet. And if so, how I may be of service to her."

Brushing the traveling dust from his trousers, he hurried toward the main entrance to the palace. More than the usual number of armed Royal Guards were posted in front and, as usual, he greeted them and continued on his way. But before he'd set one foot in the main foyer, he was surrounded by the same guards.

"Sir Edward," the head guard said with a somber expression. "The Princess Ruler has instructed me to escort you directly to her chambers upon your arrival."

"Thank you." Sir Edward nodded with relief. "Then she is here."

"Yes. And you are alone?"

"That's correct." Sir Edward removed his hat. "I wanted to

speak to the princess before I went home. I'm so sorry to hear of King Reginald's passing."

"Come at once," the guard said. "She anxiously awaits."

Sir Edward was surprised that not only the head guard, but two others—one in front and one in back—accompanied him through the great room. But it was sensible for Heather to exercise great caution during the awkward time of royal transition. She knew full well, because Sir Edward had taught her, that the short period between reigns could be fraught with unexpected peril. But as the guards led him toward the main staircase, he grew confused.

"Where are we going?" he asked the main guard.

"To the Royal Chambers," he explained.

"King Reginald's chambers?"

"The princess has taken up residence there."

"Oh, I see." Sir Edward considered this as they went up the stairs. Well, perhaps that was a wise choice too. If Princess Heather wanted to be taken seriously as queen, it was prudent to stake out her new territory, to show her strength. And could it be she found comfort amid her father's old surroundings?

Another pair of guards were positioned outside the Royal Chambers. This was beyond normal palace security. But he respected Heather's pre-emptive prudence. Perhaps she knew something he did not. Still, he couldn't fully grasp Heather making herself so much at home in her deceased father's chambers. It just didn't seem like her.

"I will announce you," the main guard informed him. Gregor

knocked on the door then quietly entered, closing the door behind him.

Unaccustomed to such formalities, Sir Edward waited. He was anxious to hear how Heather's journey had gone. And even more anxious to hear her thoughts on Michael. Had Michael revealed his identity to her yet?

"Come in," Gregor told Sir Edward, opening the door wider.

"Thank you." Sir Edward entered but was surprised that the main guard remained in the room, positioned by the door, instead of exiting and giving them privacy. Another precaution, perhaps, but was it necessary?

"Sir Edward," the princess said in a formal tone. "I am so glad you have arrived safely."

He studied her closely. "Princess *Rose*?"

Her lips curled into a chilly sort of smile. "Whom did you expect?"

"Princess Heather." He glanced around the familiar front room of the Royal Chambers, a place where he and King Reginald had enjoyed many lively conversations.

"And why is that?" Her high-necked black satin gown, which must've been quickly sewn for her father's funeral, made a swishing sound as she walked toward him.

"Because you appear to have taken up residency in the *Royal Chambers*, Princess Rose." Need he say more? Why was she here? And what did she want with him?

"You assumed my sister was here?" She waved her hand in a dismissive way. "And I assumed she was to arrive with you." Her lips puckered into a frown. "Where is she, Sir Edward? Please, assure me she has suffered no misfortune."

"She is not here yet?"

Her fair brows arched. "No. Is she expected soon?"

He tugged on his beard. "I thought she would be here ahead of me. I thought she was here now."

"Do you mean to say you were not traveling together?" She put a hand to her mouth as if shocked by this revelation. "I thought you were her guardian and protector, Sir Edward. Please, do not tell me you have left my poor sister to her own devices. What if she has come to harm?"

A wave of anxiety washed over him. *What if she had come to harm?*

"Please, Sir Edward." Rose's voice softened. "Come and sit down, dear man. You look as if you are weary and about to faint." Taking him by the arm, she led him to the seating area, calling out to her maid, "Ellen, bring us some tea. At once!"

As Sir Edward drank a few sips of tea and nibbled on a biscuit, he began to disclose some of the details of their recent adventures. Truly, what else could he do?

"You mean to tell me that my sister is out there, roaming wild lands with this strange man who—"

"He is not a strange man, Princess Rose." Sir Edward cleared his throat. "As a matter of fact, he is a prince."

Princess Rose blinked. "A prince?"

"From Mandela."

"You must be jesting with me. You cannot be suggesting that

in these few short days my sister has met up with a prince from Mandela?" She set down her cup.

"Michael promised to deliver her here." Sir Edward shook his head. "I'm sure they will arrive shortly."

"So you say. But how can I be sure? This is worrisome indeed." Rose stood, pacing back and forth, clasping and unclasping her hands.

"Perhaps they are in the palace already. Princess Heather may be in her chambers at this very moment." Sir Edward wished he felt as confident as he was trying to sound, but the truth was, he had no idea what might have become of Princess Heather. Anything might have happened out there.

"If my sister were here, I would have been notified. The Royal Guard is on high alert, watching for her arrival."

"I noticed there were many guards." Sir Edward felt sickened. Where could Princess Heather be?

"You have been an advisor to my father," Rose said in a surprisingly calm tone. "How would you advise me now?"

He tugged on his beard some more, thinking hard. "I would advise you to send out searchers. It is dangerous in the kingdom these days. Perhaps even more so now that King Reginald is departed. I would encourage you to send out large numbers of guards to find Princess Heather and deliver her safely back to the palace."

Rose nodded. "Yes, you are right. But she is disguised as a commoner. How will they recognize her?"

Now Sir Edward explained about Harry.

"You mean to tell me my sister has been gallivanting about the Raspen disguised as a *man*?" Rose shook her head. "How perverse." She studied Sir Edward. "And do I understand you to say that my sister met the prince of Mandela dressed in this outrageous costume?"

"That is correct."

"We will need more information to find her." She called out to Gregor, "Come here and take heed."

Sir Edward described in detail the clothes Heather had been wearing as well as the horse she was riding. And, pulling out his well-worn map, he pointed out the route Michael and his men planned to use to deliver Princess Heather to the palace.

Princess Rose turned to Gregor. "You heard Sir Edward. It's time to gather your most trustworthy guards. You know the ones I mean. Send them out at once." She let out an exasperated sigh. "They must not give up until they find my sister, Harry the commoner."

After the guard left, Sir Edward stood, excusing himself.

"No," Princess Rose told him. "I should like to keep you here with me for the time being."

"But I must go home and change out of traveling clothes for the king's funeral."

"We will find something suitable for you to wear here. I want you to remain in the palace as my advisor until my sister is safely returned." She gave him a beguiling look. "Do you mind?"

He was speechless. Why had she taken over the Royal

Chambers, and why was she so eager to have him as her advisor? He had never trusted Princess Rose, and something about her demeanor right now suggested she was up to no good. What was she planning?

# Chapter Twenty

About an hour before the funeral was set to begin, Heather still hadn't arrived. Sir Edward, dressed in the clean clothes provided for him, returned to the Royal Chambers as he'd been asked to do. He hoped he could send a messenger boy to his wife, informing her to meet up with him for the funeral.

As he approached the Royal Chambers, he was surprised to see even more guards posted by the door. Perhaps this was a good sign. Maybe Princess Heather had arrived. And if not, his plan was to encourage Princess Rose to postpone the king's interment until she did.

But Princess Heather was still unaccounted for, and Princess Rose was unbending, insisting it was too late to change the funeral plans.

"If you could just wait until evening," he said. "Or tomorrow morning, perhaps—"

"The coronation is scheduled for tomorrow," she said.

Sir Edward concealed his shock. "But what if Princess Heather is still detained by then?"

"You assured me she would be here by now," she reminded him. "But I'm not concerned. Even if Prince Michael fails to deliver her as you promised, it is likely the guards will have found her by then. Runners have been sent throughout the regions. By sunset, the entire kingdom will be on the lookout for *Harry*. Do not be concerned, Sir Edward. My sister will arrive here in time for the coronation."

"How can you be so certain?" He tugged on his beard. "And scheduling the coronation in such haste—well, it seems a bit premature. Why not wait for the birthday celebration, as originally planned? That would give us one more day to ensure your sister's safe arrival."

"The coronation will be tomorrow," she declared.

"And if Princess Heather is not here?"

"Then I shall assume she is not coming." Princess Rose secured the veiled hat on her head. "And in that event, I shall be ready."

"Ready?" He blinked.

"To be crowned queen." She gave him a bored expression, as if to suggest this was of little significance.

"Princess Rose, with all due respect, do you not understand the state of the kingdom right now? Are you aware there is anarchy and extreme lawlessness in the North? Do you know that war might be eminent?"

She frowned at the clock, as did he. In less than thirty minutes, the funeral procession would begin. "Sir Edward, you have been our instructor for as long as I can remember. You know as well as anyone that it is dangerous to allow a kingdom to falter between reigns. We can ill afford to let the crown sit idle, can we?"

Sir Edward shook his head. "I hope Princess Heather will be

here soon. For all we know, she may be walking through the front entrance right now."

"And if she is not?" Princess Rose stood, checking to be sure her mourning veil covered her face.

"Then she will be here soon. I believe it."

"And if she is *not?*" She glared through her veil at him. "I cannot be held to blame for my sister's bad timing and irresponsibility." She tapped him on the chest. "Can you make the same claim?"

"Perhaps not. But you still don't understand something, Princess Rose. Something important regarding the kingdom— and the person who would rule it. With all due respect, Princess, I beg you to listen to reason." He told her, in specific detail, about the true state of the kingdom, even explaining how the people were ready to welcome Queen Heather.

She waved her hand. "Yes, I know all is not well in the kingdom. But I haven't time for this, Sir Edward."

"You must listen to me. The only hope I have for your father's kingdom to endure is for your sister to be crowned queen. And I fear that if you attempt to take the throne, chaos will erupt. And you, dear Princess, will be in grave danger."

From behind her veil, her blue eyes flashed in anger. "That is no way to speak to your future queen!" Before he could answer, she called out to the pair of guards standing just inside the door. "Escort Sir Edward to the special chamber you have prepared for him. Now!"

"But the funeral," he said as a pair of guards took him firmly by each arm. "It's about to begin."

"You will not attend the funeral." Princess Rose narrowed her eyes at him.

The guards escorted him out of the chambers, immediately joined by two more. Instead of walking him toward the main staircase, they took him down a dark hallway and down another staircase. Sir Edward was acquainted with this route. It was only used for two purposes. To make a hasty retreat in the event of an attack, if one turned to the right. Or to go down to the dungeons, if one turned to the left. As they turned left and started to descend the steep and dimly lit stairs, he knew where he was going.

"Why are you doing this?" he demanded as they shoved him into a damp, dark cell. "This is wrong!"

"Just following orders," one said gruffly. And with a loud clang, the door was slammed shut and the guards hurried away, leaving the youngest one behind to keep watch.

"Do you understand the folly of what you have done?" With his hands on the bars of the small window, Sir Edward pleaded with the young guard.

"Please, be quiet," the guard said politely. "It will be better for you."

Sir Edward peered curiously at the young man. "Do I know you?"

"Aye. You used to know me, sir."

Sir Edward studied his ruddy cheeks and thick sandy hair. "You're Thomas Miller's boy, are you not? Thomas Junior?"

"I go by Thomas now. My dad passed away last year."

"I was quite fond of your father. He had been with the Royal Guard for many years. The king had been quite fond of him too."

"Aye. And my dad was devoted to the king." Thomas sighed as he pulled a wooden stool away from the wall and sat down. "I'm disappointed I can't attend the king's funeral."

"So am I." Sir Edward sighed.

"If we listen, we may hear the trumpets." Thomas crooked a hand to his ear. "I think that's them now, sir."

For a while they both waited in silence, and although Sir Edward's ears were not sharp enough to hear the trumpets, he knew just how they would sound. Sir Edward had always had a good imagination, which he wondered if it might come in useful down here.

"I can imagine what it must be like at the funeral." He spoke with a quiet intensity, using the storyteller tone that he sometimes employed to entice his students toward education.

"Truly?" Thomas looked up hopefully.

Sir Edward began to describe the way he could envision the solemn procession. "They will assemble out by the Royal Stables first," he began. "Some of the higher royal guard will lead the way carrying the flags and dressed in their best uniforms." He looked at Thomas. "How long have you been in the Royal Guard, son?"

"It'll be a year this summer. I got my appointment after my dad passed on. I'm only in the lower guards and wouldn't be involved in, well, *this*, if Princess Rose hadn't liked the looks of me." He gave an embarrassed smile as he ran his hand through his sandy curls. "Please, tell me more about the funeral, Sir Edward. I want to pretend I am there."

Sir Edward described how the musicians would follow the guards, playing sad but regal notes on the trumpets, and how the sound of the drum would be muffled and mournful. "Next comes the team of six black horses pulling the open carriage where the king's casket, draped in the Raspen coat of arms and visible for all to see, will be displayed. After that will come King Reginald's horse, wearing the king's empty saddle and the king's sword hanging in its sheath, never to be used again."

"I can almost see it," Thomas said wistfully.

"After that, the Royal Carriage will arrive Princess Rose. Truly, it should be both princesses in the carriage, but sadly that is not the case." Sir Edward watched Thomas's expression, trying to determine if the young man even cared.

"Normally, the head of the Royal Council should be seated in the same carriage, but Princess Heather informed me that King Reginald had dismissed Sir Rupert several days ago. Is that true?"

"I heard there had been some changes in the council, but I really can't say."

*Can't or won't?* Sir Edward wondered. He continued describing the procession, clear down to the last of it, then sighed. "I almost feel I were there."

"Me too." Thomas brightened a bit. "Thank you, sir."

"You seem a good fellow," Sir Edward said cautiously. "And your father was a good fellow. Are you not concerned about your alliance with Princess Rose?"

"Not if she is to rule the kingdom."

"Do you not understand that when Princess Heather comes home, she will take her rightful throne? And then I will be released from here and appointed as head of the Royal Council. Can you not see how the guards involved in my unlawful imprisonment will be held responsible?"

"Princess Heather will never be crowned queen," the guard said glumly. "Not really."

"How can you know that?"

"Never mind."

"Talk to me, son," Sir Edward pleaded. "Perhaps when Princess Heather gets back to the palace, I can help you."

"It is Princess Heather who will need help." He looked away. "I mean the *real* one."

"The real what?"

"The real Princess Heather."

"Thomas, I spoke clearly and plainly to you. Why do you not speak in a similar manner to me?"

Thomas shrugged then got up from his stool and, coming closer, he lowered his voice as if he thought someone might be listening, although there appeared to be no one else down here. "I always liked Princess Heather, sir. Better than her sister. But she will never be queen."

"Please, tell me how you can be so certain." Sir Edward made a cautious smile. "You know I can be trusted, son. Besides, who would I tell?"

"Aye. You are going nowhere, sir."

"So tell me what you know. And if I ever have the chance, I will repay you. Or at the very least, I will tell you more stories. In the case you are stuck with me for a while, it could help to pass the time."

Thomas nodded. "The guards are out looking for Princess

Heather right now. They say she's dressed like a fellow. When she is found, they are instructed to bring her back here, where she will be imprisoned. Just like you. After that, I don't know her fate."

"What if they don't find her?"

"They will. Everyone in the kingdom is looking for the man by the name of Harry. There is a reward on Harry's head. He is wanted 'dead or alive.' If you get my meaning."

"Oh." Sir Edward felt sickened. "Is there nothing to be done?"

"It has already been done. Princess Rose has seen to everything."

Sir Edward sunk down onto the stool in his cell and, holding his head in his hands, wept like a baby. Some of his tears were for the king, and many were for the realization that he might never see his beloved wife or his son again, but his most bitter tears were for Princess Heather and the unfortunate fate of the kingdom.

# Chapter Twenty-One

Heather opened her eyes to unfamiliar surroundings. However, she was snugly wrapped in quilts and blankets and felt surprisingly warm and dry. Nearby, a cheerful fire crackled in the stone fireplace. As she sat up, the last thing she could recall was drowning in the river. *Was this heaven?*

"Are you awake, miss?"

Heather looked over to spy an old woman pushing herself from a rocking chair and slowly walking toward her.

"Who are you?" Heather asked.

"Maggie," the old woman said.

"Where am I?" Heather stared as the small, white-haired woman came closer. With her wrinkled, spotty skin and pale gray eyes, she looked to be about a hundred years old.

"You are in my humble home." Maggie fluffed a pillow and slipped it behind Heather's back. "Let me get you some warm milk, dear."

"How did I get here?"

"Your friend brought you to me." Maggie handed her a chipped china mug with violets on it. "Drink this up. You need to regain your strength."

153

Heather took a hesitant sniff. After all, this old woman was a stranger, and for all Heather knew, she might be a witch. But when she tasted it, the milk was sweet, as if honey had been added, as well as a touch of cinnamon. Heather finished it to the last drop then handed it back. "Thank you, Maggie."

"You are most welcome." She peered into Heather's face. "I thought you were a boy when they carried you in. I was a bit surprised to discover you were a girl."

Heather made an uneasy smile. "It's safer to travel as a boy than as a girl."

"Aye. Sensible indeed. A girl wouldn't be safe traveling about the countryside these days. And now I will dish you up some broth. I made it this morning, and if I do say so myself, it's good. I already had my supper."

"I still don't understand how I got here." Heather peered down at her clothing, surprised to discover she was wearing a white flannel nightgown. "The last thing I remember was drowning in the Serpentine River. Or very nearly drowning. How did I get from there to here?"

"Your friend brought you to me," Maggie said again. "Poor thing, you were half frozen and nearly dead."

"What friend?" Heather wondered about Sir Edward and Luther. Had they rescued her?

"Your friend Michael."

"Michael?" Heather frowned. "Michael brought me here?"

"Aye. That's right. Michael and some other fellows. Along with my grandson."

"This Michael...do you know him?"

"I never met him before. He's a friend of my grandson."

"What did Michael look like?"

Maggie grinned, revealing some missing teeth. "Oh, he was a fine looking fellow indeed. Tall and handsome, with sparkling eyes and dark, curly hair. Well-mannered too. He seemed quite fond of you. Is he not your young man?"

Heather blinked. "You say he was with friends. Was this Michael with a man called Sir Jonathan?"

"No, I don't recall that name. There were three men including my grandson. But you should know this. Were they not friends of yours?"

"Your grandson?" she questioned. "What is his name?"

"That would be Garret."

"Garret?" Heather was even more confused. "Is he tall with fair hair?"

"That's right. I hadn't seen dear Garret in years. I would not have recognized him had he not looked so like his father." She sighed. "So grand to see him after all this time. He ventured away from home when he was a young man. Now he has a wife and three grown children. Imagine!"

"And another man named Martin?"

"Yes, now you're remembering just fine." Maggie held out a bowl of broth. "Eat this, and perhaps you will begin to feel more like yourself again."

Heather felt bamboozled. Michael was connected to Garret and Martin, the men who had kidnapped her from the gypsy camp? What did this mean? Was Michael not to be trusted?

"Come now, dear. Be a good girl and eat your broth."

Heather dipped the spoon into the bowl, taking a cautious sip. Was this old woman truly trustworthy? But the broth tasted good, and Heather was hungry. "How long have I been here?"

"They brought you yesterday. In the afternoon."

"And what time is it now? Do you know?"

"I don't know the exact time, but it's been dark outside for awhile. You slept for quite a spell. I feared you'd never wake up. But I 'spect you needed the rest."

Heather tried to absorb all this. She'd been here one night already, and now it was the second night. "What happened to your grandson and the others?"

"They had to attend to some business, but they promised to come back for you. I thought they may have been here by now. Perhaps tomorrow."

"Do you know what happened to my horse? Did they leave him here for me?"

Maggie's brow creased. "Your horse? No, I don't recall any mention of your horse. Although the three men were all on horseback. But, no, they left no horse behind."

Heather set the empty bowl in her lap as a hard lump filled her throat. She knew it was foolish to cry for a horse. So many things she could've wept for these past few days, it seemed childish to shed tears for an animal. Yet she couldn't help herself. Zephyr was a good, loyal horse, and she had loved him dearly. She never should've forced him into that river. It was her fault he didn't survive.

"Are you crying, child?" The old woman stooped over to pick up the bowl. "Why are you sad?"

Heather wiped her tears with her hands. "No, I'm fine."

"I 'spect there will be a few tears spilled by now."

Heather sniffed. "Why is that?"

"Oh, you could not have heard the news." The woman was back at the table, cutting a generous slice of bread.

"What news?"

"My neighbor stopped by just before the sun went down. She's the one that brought me this bread." Maggie slathered some butter and jam onto the bread, carrying it over to Heather.

"Thank you." Heather took an eager bite of the bread and butter. "What news did your neighbor bring?"

"Oh, yes, Olivia. She's a widow like me. We look in on each other and share food sometimes. A good woman, she is. Don't know what I'd do without her."

"She sounds like a good neighbor. You say she brought news?"

"We do depend on our neighbors, way out here away from everything."

"Where are we? Where is it you live?"

"You're in the Borderlands, dear." Maggie made a wistful smile. "My husband, God rest his soul, moved us out here long ago. He thought Westside was overcrowded, and he wanted to make a home out here." She waved her hand. "He built us this cottage."

"How far are we from Westside?"

"Oh, it's a good day's walk from here. I used to go sometimes. But not for many years."

"But what about the news you mentioned?" Heather ate the last bite of bread. "Did you say it was sad?"

"Sad for some. Not for everyone. My neighbor's son just got

back from Westside. He heard the news there." She shook her head. "He says the king is dead."

Heather stared at Maggie. "What?"

"Aye. They say he died in his sleep. Not last night, but the night before that. They will bury him on the morrow."

"The king is dead?" Heather said the words, trying to grasp this sorrowful news as tears filled her eyes.

"Aye. I know I should be sadder." Maggie was cleaning up the supper things now, her back to Heather as she rambled. "But maybe it's for the best. From what I hear, he has not been a good leader for Raspen. Not for many a year. Perhaps it's time for a change. Anyway, that's what folks over in Westside say. So I 'spect they know."

Heather turned her face to the fire, the tears rolling freely down her cheeks, as the old woman continued to chatter on about how the kingdom used to be run so much better by the previous king, Heather's grandfather, a man she never had known.

All Heather could think was that her father was dead—gone for good—and she would never see him again. *Never!* And his funeral was tomorrow? How could that be? She had to get home as quickly as possible. Not only for the sake of the kingdom, which was probably in chaos, but to get away before Michael and his band of kidnapping bullies returned.

She felt a wave of panic. What would happen to her if they arrived before she could escape? She knew that Michael had betrayed her confidence, revealing her identity to his beastly friends. It was possible that even this old woman was in the know, although she seemed oblivious.

Heather remembered her father's ring. Fearing it had been taken, she fumbled with the neck of the flannel nightgown. Someone had removed her wet clothes. What if they had seen it and confiscated it? Finding the chain, Heather tugged it up and, feeling the shape of the ring, let out a relieved sigh.

"I appreciate your hospitality," she told Maggie. The old woman had returned to her rocking chair where she appeared to be sewing something by the light of an oil lamp. "Someday I hope I can repay you for your kindness."

Maggie waved her hand. "No need for that, dear. Michael has taken care of everything for you. Good man, that Michael. I'm grateful that he and my Garret are friends. One needs good friends."

With Maggie occupied with her sewing, Heather studied her surroundings, memorizing the lay of furniture and where the door was located. She spotted her boots by the fireplace, and her clothes draped over a chair right next to them. She hoped they would be dry, but even if they weren't, she would leave. She would be out of here at the first opportunity. With luck, after Maggie went to sleep. When would that be?

Heather looked down at the narrow cot she occupied. "Oh, Maggie, I hope I haven't taken your bed or your bedding."

"No worries, dear. That's a spare bed you're in. We moved it out by the fire here to keep you warm. You were so cold when they brung you inside—your skin was the color of a foggy day."

"Thank you for helping me." Heather lay back down. "And if you don't mind, I think I will rest some more. The food and the fire are making me sleepy."

"Aye. Get your rest, dear. I'll just put another log on the fire and finish up this mending, and then I'll be off to bed myself."

"Goodnight, Maggie." Heather closed her eyes, biding her time until she was certain that Maggie was asleep. But what she said was true. The food and the fire had made her sleepy, and soon she was drifting off.

When Heather awoke, the lantern was out, and the old woman was snoring. Heather climbed out of bed and tiptoed over to the chair with her clothes. By the dim light of the red coals in the fireplace, she put her clothes on over the flannel nightgown. Once she returned to the palace, she would send a messenger back here with it, along with a gift for Maggie. Until then, it would help keep her warm.

Finally dressed, with her hair pinned in place as best she could do with only two hairpins that she'd found in a pocket, she was ready to leave. She paused to ensure Maggie was still snoring. She did not want to disturb the old woman's sleep, nor did she want Maggie to have any idea when she'd left. In case she tipped off Michael.

Heather tiptoed over to the door, praying that it would be a clear night outside. She needed the stars to guide her eastward, toward Westside. Holding her breath, she slipped the door's latch open, cringing as it let out a small squeak, but hearing Maggie's even snores, she continued out.

As she closed the door, she saw that not only was the sky clear, but there was a nearly full moon coming up in the trees. That must be east, she told herself. Although the bright moon made it more difficult to see the stars, she spotted the North Star.

Using the stars and the moon as her compass, she began to walk. Heather knew it wasn't realistic that she would reach Westside before daybreak, but if she could just put some distance between herself and the cottage, she would feel better.

The moon helped to light her path as Heather picked her way through the woods. Fortunately, these woods weren't as rough or thickly forested as the Wilderness, but it was still slow going. She had to stop regularly to peer up at the sky, spot the North Star, and continue toward where she hoped she would come to Westside. As she walked, she thought of her father, remembering all the good times she had shared with him growing up. Much of the time, especially after the queen died, he had treated Heather like a son. He'd indulged her desires to use a bow and a sword and to fight. And he'd taught her to ride. It seemed impossible to think he was dead—that he'd died two nights ago, and she hadn't even known it.

It shamed her to think that while her father had been on his deathbed, she'd been dancing around the campfire with the gypsies. What kind of daughter was she? Did she even deserve to inherit the throne? On the other hand, what would happen if Heather never made it home? Where would the kingdom be if Princess Rose were crowned queen? These were the thoughts that kept Heather moving.

She had to get home.

# Chapter Twenty-Two

Princess Rose was nobody's fool. Certainly, there were those who believed she wasn't as smart as her sister and unsuitable to rule as queen, but Rose knew better. Simply because her sister had been lucky enough to emerge from the womb first was no reason she should get all this. Rose looked around at what used to be her father's chambers, deciding that one of her first queenly duties, after tomorrow's coronation, would be to call in the Royal Decorators and ask them to redo everything in here. She wanted new upholstery, new drapes, new tables and lamps, and art befitting a queen. But right now, there were other fish to fry.

"You called for me, Your Highness?"

"Yes, Clara." Rose patted the couch next to her. "Come and sit with me."

"Sit with you?" Clara blinked in wonder. "Me?"

"Yes, yes. Hurry, Clara, I have much to discuss and little time to do it."

The yellow-haired servant girl sat down on the edge of the couch and, with wide eyes, listened as Rose described her plan.

"I'm not sure I understand." Clara looked confused.

"It's simple. You couldn't have an easier job. All you need do is remain in my chambers and lie in my fine bed and eat my delicious food and wear my clothes. But you must hide your face if anyone other than my trusted handmaids enters the room. You must pretend you are me but that you are sick with grief. Do you grasp my meaning?"

"I think I do."

"Let me see how well you can do at crying."

Clara made a sobbing sound, holding her hands over her face.

"That's not bad but work on it."

"I will, Your Highness."

"It's an important job. You cannot let me down. Do you comprehend what I need you to do?"

Clara beamed at her. "Yes, Your Highness. I do."

"And if you fail me"—Rose narrowed her eyes—"you will be put to death. Do you understand that?"

Clara's smile faded. "Yes, Your Highness."

"I have chosen you because I believe you are trustworthy." Rose reached for a curl of Clara's hair, giving it a friendly tug. "And because of your lovely golden locks."

"Thank you, Your Highness. I will do just as you have asked. I give you my word."

Rose smiled. "And you do not wonder why I ask such a strange thing of you?"

Clara's mouth twisted to one side. "Aye, Your Highness, I do wonder."

"For the time being, I will be Princess Heather. I will be crowned as queen tomorrow. And I will celebrate my birthday on the following day. I will make excuses for Princess Rose. I will say she is too grief stricken to attend. And no one will know I am not my sister. Even now, the rumor is spreading that Princess Heather has returned to the palace. Do you get my meaning?"

"I'm not sure. Has Princess Heather returned?"

"No. But even if she does, I will deal with it. You see, I am the one who should be queen. I will be crowned as Queen Heather. And I will rule as Queen Heather. During this time, you will play Princess Rose—the daughter who is grieving for her father and who cannot leave her chambers. I will make Rose's excuses, and I will gather sympathy for the poor, devoted Rose. And then— after enough time has passed—Queen Heather." Rose pointed to herself. "She will grow deathly ill with a horrible, disfiguring disease, to which she will succumb, poor thing."

"Oh my!" Clara gasped. "That is awful."

"No, Princess Heather won't really be sick like that. It's all simply a hoax, my dear. And then, of course, Princess Rose will be next in line for the throne. And that means I can return to being me again." Rose laughed. "Of course, that is when your job of imitating me comes to a swift end. No more sleeping in my bed and eating my food. But not to worry, you will be rewarded for your loyalty. Trust me."

"So you will be crowned queen twice?" Clara blinked. "Once as Queen Heather and once as Queen Rose?"

"That is correct." Rose patted her on the head. "And just think. You will be a part of all this."

"Oh, Your Highness, I am so honored."

Rose smiled as Clara hurried off to meet the handmaid who was already privy to Rose's brilliant scheme and awaiting Clara's arrival. The yellow-haired servant girl might not feel so honored when it was time to switch roles and play that of the dearly departed Queen Heather. But someone had to fill the casket for the royal funeral. And to think there were some in the kingdom who did not think Rose was the smarter sister.

Fully aware that Heather would not have anything as stylish as Rose's black satin mourning gown, Rose had sent one of her handmaids to fetch something suitable from Heather's chambers. Her handmaids—she had limited herself to two—were just finishing helping her into the plain silk gown in a somber shade of charcoal gray, when there was a knock on the door.

"Go see who that is," Rose told Margot. "And remember that I am Princess Heather. If they are asking for Princess Rose, explain what has happened."

"Yes, Your Highness, I know what I'm to say. Princess Rose has taken to her bed in her own chambers. Princess Heather is occupying the Royal Chamber because she will be crowned queen tomorrow."

"Good girl." Rose smiled.

While Margot tended to the door, the second handmaid went to work rearranging Rose's hair. "Remember to keep it plain and simple, Alice. I know it's boring, but I need to look like Heather."

"Aye, Your Highness. I remember how Mindy did Princess Heather's hair. Not much to it. I never envied Mindy's position. Especially since your sister insisted on keeping only one handmaid."

"Mindy will be working in the kitchen soon." Rose chuckled to imagine the handmaid's face when "Queen Heather" had demoted her to a scullery maid. Especially considering how Mindy acted a bit uppity at times. As if she thought she was better than the other maids simply because Heather treated her as a friend. Mindy, she hoped, would tire of scrubbing pots and pans and decide to leave the palace altogether.

Margot returned to the dressing room with an alarmed expression. "Excuse me, mum, it's a young gentleman named Michael. He says he's here to see Princess Heather, and he seems to think she will want to see him."

"Michael?" Rose stood up from the dressing table. "The prince from Mandela?"

"He did not say he was a prince, Your Highness, but he has a regal look to him."

"He is handsome?"

"Oh, yes, Your Highness." Margot giggled.

"And Heather did not come here with him? You are certain of this?"

"That was my impression. The gentleman seems eager to see her—I mean *you*, Princess Heather. He said that he had heard she's back in the palace."

Rose nodded. The rumor mill was already at work. But she felt a bit nervous now. Was she really ready for this stunt? Just how well did this Michael know Heather? And how much did he know? Well, there was only one way to find out. "Invite him into the sitting room, Margot."

"Yes, Your Highness."

"Tell him I will be out shortly." Rose looked into the dressing table mirror, frowning at the drab gray gown that had been foraged from her sister's wardrobe. The black satin had been much more stylish. But she needed to focus on becoming Heather. She had to think like Heather and act like Heather. Convincing this young man would be Rose's first real test—would she be able to pass?

As Alice put the last hairpin into the simple hairstyle, Rose took in a deep breath. The key to playing Heather would be to think and act in the opposite way that she would do as Rose. For instance, where Rose was talkative, Heather would be quiet. Where Rose would flirt with an attractive man, Heather would be standoffish. Perhaps this wasn't so difficult after all.

Rose assumed the regal posture that befitted a queen then stopped herself. Heather was much more casual in her posture, a tendency that Rose found irritating. Still, if she were to pass for Heather, she would need to be mindful of all her sister's aggravating habits. Hopefully, in time, people would come to accept that "Queen Heather" carried herself with more poise and dignity. And after a month or so of being queen, she might start to dress a bit more fashionably and maybe even allow the royal hairdresser to style her hair with more elegance. In time, it could happen.

Rose paused by the heavy velvet curtain that separated the sitting room from the rest of the Royal Chamber, peeking out to see the dark-haired young man standing nervously by the fireplace. She was glad to see he was uneasy. That would give her the upper hand.

"Michael," she said as she entered the room. "Sorry to keep you waiting."

"Oh, Heather," he exclaimed, rushing toward her. "It's so good to see you. I've been so worried. How did you get here?"

Without speaking, she studied his face. He *was* handsome. Not in the fair-haired, blue-eyed way she had hoped he might be. But he was tall and strong, and his dark curly hair and brown eyes had a certain appeal. Was he truly a prince?

"I don't blame you for being angry at me, Heather. I'm so sorry I left you behind at Maggie's. But I knew she'd take good care of you until I returned. And then you were gone. Why did you leave like that?"

Rose shook her head and turned away, pretending to be interested in the crackling fire but trying to think of a response.

"I'm sorry," he said again. "Here I am going on and on, and I haven't even expressed my sincere sympathy." He placed his hand on her shoulder in a familiar way. "I just heard the news of your father. I am so sorry for your loss."

She turned back to face him, feigning deep sadness. "Yes, it was a great shock. I didn't even get here in time for his funeral."

"I truly am sorry. I know how much you loved your father. And I remember how I spoke disparagingly of him the night we first met. I offer you my most sincere apology."

Rose let out a long sigh. "Well, that was then."

"So, you forgive me for all my careless words?"

She folded her arms across her front, just how Heather often did when contemplating something.

"Please, tell me you forgive me, Heather. I will not have peace until you do."

"Fine." She nodded with a grim expression. "I forgive you. Please, speak of it no more."

"Thank you." He made a relieved sigh. "You are gracious."

She tipped her head to one side, the way her sister did when she was curious. "Tell me, Michael, why have you come here?"

He blinked. "To see you, of course. To make certain you are well. I had promised to get you back here safely." He gazed down to the floor. "And I failed."

"But I am here," she pointed out.

He looked up with bright eyes. "Yes! You are. And I'm so glad you are. It truly is good to see you. How are Sir Edward and Luther?"

Rose weighed her words. "I only just arrived, Michael. I have not seen them yet, but I'm sure they are fine and happy to be home."

"Yes, of course." He reached over to take her hand, squeezing. "You look so different, Heather."

"Different?" Rose tried to stay calm. "What do you mean?"

He grinned. "Seeing you like this, dressed like a woman. I suppose I expected to see you dressed like Harry." He laughed. "You don't look like the fellow I tussled with in the cave."

Rose pulled her hand from him, once again turning away.

"I'm sorry, Heather. I didn't mean to embarrass you."

"It's just that...well, I'm sure you've heard...tomorrow I will be crowned queen. I must conduct myself as such. Surely you understand." She turned to see his reaction. "I'm no longer that person you met gallivanting about the kingdom."

"I understand. Speaking of gallivanting, I brought your horse with me. I left him at the stables."

"Oh." She nodded. "Thank you."

He gave her a curious look, and she felt a bit uneasy.

"So, you came to see if I made it back. If I am well." She gave him a shy smile. "Is that all?"

His eyes lit up again. "I don't want that to be all."

"Oh?"

"There's something I didn't tell you, Heather."

"Yes?"

"When we were being honest with each other, after the cave, I failed to be forthcoming. Perhaps in more way than one."

"What do you mean?" She tipped her head to one side, putting a winsome look on her face and waiting.

"I didn't tell you my real connection to Mandela."

"And that would be?"

He came close to her again, grasping both of her hands in his. "My father is king, Heather. I am a prince."

She pretended to be surprised.

"But I am not heir to the kingdom."

"But your father is king?"

"Yes. But I have an older brother. He will follow my father's reign."

"Oh. I see." With her hands still nestled in his, Rose tried to grasp the meaning of this. Michael was a prince but would not be king. This was unexpected, but it could be beneficial—to everyone involved. An alliance with Mandela would strengthen both kingdoms.

"But you said you weren't forthcoming in other ways, Michael. What did you mean by that?"

"I mean that I had feelings for you, Heather. I have been thinking about you ever since that, uh, that kiss."

"Oh?" She looked directly into his eyes now. "You know, I've never been to Mandela."

"We could easily remedy that." He grinned. "You must know why I'm here, Heather, besides wanting to be sure you were safely home." He got down on one knee, still holding both her hands in his and looking up at her with adoring eyes. "Heather, my darling, please tell me you will become my wife."

"Yes!" she exclaimed triumphantly. As he stood, eagerly gathering her into his arms and kissing her, Rose knew she had won!

# Chapter Twenty-Three

When the clear sky turned to fog, Heather knew it was time to rest. To walk in the fog without a compass was asking for trouble. Finding a grove of oaks, she curled up against a thick tree trunk and fell asleep.

She woke to the light but was dismayed to see the fog was still there. However, as she studied the sky, she was certain it was brighter on one side. That had to be the east. And that was the direction she walked toward.

Still grieving her father and berating herself for ever wanting to go out on this silly expedition, she fixed her sights on the eastern sky, which was growing steadily brighter. Just as the fog parted and the sun broke through with a golden warmth that was most welcome, she remembered that last moment in the Serpentine River—the instant when she thought death had been imminent.

With clarity, she remembered how her father had been there to meet her—with arms outstretched, his smile had been bigger than any she recalled during his life. And she'd been deliriously happy to see him, racing toward him.

Heather paused, soaking in the warmth of the morning sun

as realization hit her. That must've been her father's way of telling her goodbye. That had to be it.

"Goodbye, dear Father," she said aloud. "I know I will see you again someday. Hopefully not too soon." She looked up at the sky. "Because there's work to be done down here first. And I intend to do it."

According to the angle of the sun, it was midafternoon by the time Heather reached the outskirts of Westside. The soles of her riding boots had worn paper thin, and her feet were throbbing in pain. She wasn't even sure she had the strength to walk all the way through town in search of a guard.

That was her plan. Find a guard and confess her identity— she would even show them the royal ring if necessary. Once she gained their confidence, she would command them to deliver her to the palace—at once. She knew it was impossible to make it to Southside in time for her father's funeral. In all likelihood, it was already over and done. But with help from the Royal Guard, she would be there before sunrise tomorrow.

"Harry!"

Heather turned at the sound of that name. Was it in reference to her—or someone whose name was truly Harry? She spotted the village woman in a simple brown dress, waving her arms frantically as she hurried toward her. As she came close, Heather recognized the auburn hair and bright green eyes.

"Bess?" Heather tugged her hat down, hoping that her braided hair had stayed put during the night. "Is that really you?"

"Aye, 'tis me." Bess paused to catch her breath. "And you must come with me. Now!"

Heather blinked. "Wait, I—"

"No time to wait." Bess linked her arm in Heather's. "You are in grave danger."

"What do you mean?" Heather's feet ached as she tried to keep up with Bess's fast pace.

"My mum's house is down this street," Bess told her. "We must hurry."

"What is—"

"There is a warrant," Bess told her. "For you, Harry. There's a price on your head, and everyone is on the lookout for you."

"A warrant? A price on my head?"

"They says you're a threat to the kingdom, Harry. That you're a dangerous man. But I knows it can't be true."

"Of course that's not true."

"I seen Sir Edward and Luther at the inn. Just yesterday. I asked them to give you my regards. Sir Edward told me you would be saddened to hear of the king's death." She glanced at Heather. "I wish I hadn't spoken the way I did when we first met. I knows you had great respect for the king, Harry."

"Yes, I do. It was distressing to hear he had passed."

"His funeral probably is over. But the village is crawling with them guards—all looking for you." She peered curiously at him. "Why are they wanting you so badly? And here with the king barely in his grave. Did you do something terrible bad, Harry?"

"No." Heather shook her head.

"Here we are." Bess tugged Heather up to the door of a small stone cottage. "Get inside quick. Afore anyone sees you."

Looking forward to sitting down and resting her feet, Heather didn't argue as she hurried into the house, waiting for Bess to close and secure the door.

"This is my Harry," Bess called out. "Come and meet him, Mum." She turned to Harry. "My mum's name is Jane."

A woman who looked like an older version of Bess emerged from the shadows. Her eyes were the same emerald green, but her auburn hair was duller and tinged with gray. And her expression was grim.

"Pleased to meet you, ma'am." Heather politely tipped her head.

"Oh, Bess." Jane wrung her hands. "Why have you brought him here?"

"What else could I do? Let him get taken by the guards and strung up like a criminal?" She turned to Heather. "You're not a criminal, are you?"

"No." Heather sank down onto a wooden stool. "I certainly am not."

"Then why is there a warrant for your arrest?" Jane demanded. "Why is the town being turned upside down and inside out with everyone searching for you?"

Heather looked at Bess. "I don't know."

"There must be a reason," Jane insisted. "Did you have something to do with the king's death?"

The words cut to Heather's heart—for the truth was, she had wondered about this. If Heather had been home, would her father be dead? But then she remembered the warm golden vision she'd had of him. She shook her head. "No, I did not."

"Then why are they offering such a reward for your capture?"

Jane challenged. "Tell me that if you can. And while you're at it, Harry, tell me why we shouldn't turn you in and collect the reward ourselves." She waved her hand to the table behind her. "We are nearly out of food as it is, and we're not likely to make a penny selling my knit goods—not with all the goings on in the kingdom right now, what with the king's funeral and all the fuss over the coronation tomorrow—"

"The coronation's tomorrow?"

"Aye." Bess nodded. "Have you not heard?"

"Who is to become queen?"

"It's a terrible upset. They say Princess Rose is taking the crown because Princess Heather has gone missing. They fear poor Princess Heather may be dead."

"No." Heather shook her head. "That's not true."

"That's it!" Jane pointed her finger at Harry. "You've had something to do with Princess Heather. Did you kidnap her? Murder her?" Jane rushed past Heather toward the door. "I'm calling the guard."

"Stop!" Heather put a firm hand on Jane's arm.

"Please, Harry," Bess cried. "Don't hurt my mum. I begs you."

"Just wait a minute." Heather used her normal, higher-pitched voice now. "Everyone calm down, and I will tell you the truth."

Jane turned around, peering at Heather. "What is going on here? Are you a man or a woman?"

Heather pulled off her hat and, shaking her hair, which had only been loosely in place, sheepishly smile. "I am a woman."

Bess gasped and reached for a stool, lowering herself down with a shocked expression. "Oh! My! Goodness!"

"That's not all of the truth." Heather took Jane by the arm and, leading her over to a chair, she helped her sit down. "I am going to believe that I can trust you both." She reached down below her layers of clothing, fishing out the royal ring. "I am Princess Heather. This is the king's sign to prove my identity. I am heir to the throne, and I must get to the palace as soon as possible." She held the sapphire and diamond ring close enough for both Bess and her mother to thoroughly examine it. In the next instant, both women fell to their knees.

"Please," Heather said. "Get up. We don't have much time. And I need your help."

"Your Highness, please, may I ask you a question?" Jane said.

"Certainly."

"Why are you dressed as a man?"

Heather explained her story, watching with a bit of amusement as both Jane and Bess's eyes grew wide with wonder.

"I thought there was something fishy about you," Bess declared. "I mean, I'm sorry, Your Highness. I didn't mean to sound fresh. Please, forgive me."

"Never mind," Heather told her. "Will you both help me?"

"Yes." Jane nodded firmly. "However we can. We're happy to help you. But we are poor and—"

"That's no matter," Heather assured her. "First of all, I'll need another disguise. I can't go around dressed as Harry anymore."

"That's for sure and for certain." Bess nodded then frowned. "But why have they placed a price on your head? I mean on Harry's head?"

"I'm afraid that is my sister's doing. She wants to be queen."

"Your sister sounds evil." Bess clapped her hand over her mouth. "I'm sorry. I shouldn't have said—"

"No, you're partially right. But I'm not sure if she's evil or just plain stupid to think she can pull this off."

"We don't have much to offer in the way of a disguise," Jane told Heather. "Only our own clothes."

"That will be perfect." She pointed at Jane. "If I can dress similar to you and pretend to be an older woman, I should be able to blend with the crowd." Heather looked at Bess. "And if I had a young female traveling companion, I could pretend to be her mother."

"You do not look like my mother, Princess Heather."

"You both shall assist me to look like a mother."

With the help of Bess, and with Jane's dark blue Sunday dress, brown shawl, white bonnet, and heavy black shoes, along with some ashes from the fireplace that transformed Heather's hair to gray and dulled her complexion, she was ready.

"Helping me make my way to the palace may be risky," she told Jane. "If you would rather Bess not go, I will understand."

"I am going," Bess insisted.

Jane rolled her eyes. "My daughter is a stubborn one. Who can stop her?"

"I give you my word, you will both be rewarded. When I am queen."

Jane's countenance softened. "Our reward will be that you—and not your sister—sits on the throne. That will be enough."

Heather grasped her hand. "You are a good woman."

"God go with you," Jane said as she opened the door.

Heather and Bess slipped out, and they were soon mixing with the throngs of people filling the streets in the central part of the village. Everyone was merry, as if today were a holiday. And perhaps it was for them. Heather, though weary, had a strong suspicion that her work had only just begun.

Before long, thanks to Bess's outgoing nature, the two travelers posing as mother and daughter were invited to ride on an oxen-pulled wagon. Filled with jovial farm peasants, these merrymakers were in route to Southside, where they planned to enjoy the festivities of the upcoming coronation and birthday celebration. While Bess chatted with the sojourners, Heather played the old woman, bowing her head and pretending to snooze…and, bone-weary from last night's long trek, she soon fell asleep.

# Chapter Twenty-Four

Heather tried to act natural, holding Bess's hand as she walked up to the servants' door of the palace. Due to the coronation ceremony, which probably was finished by now, and due to a certain young "criminal" named Harry, the guards had been all over the place today. As they approached the servant's door, she was being watched by a pair of the lower guards.

"I'm 'ere to bring my girl for service," Heather said in what she hoped sounded like the voice of an old village woman. "Mrs. Eunice sent a message to bring Bess round this evening. Seems the palace is shorthanded for all the festivities." She sniffed loudly and wiped her nose with the back of her hand.

Bess batted her eyelashes at the young guards. "It must be great fun to work in the palace—what with you handsome guards about." She giggled. "I feel so safe."

"Go on in," a guard told Heather. "But don't be dillydallying about. We don't want a bunch of extra folks under foot right."

"Thank you, young man." Heather nodded. "I'll just find Mrs. Eunice and be on my way." She grabbed Bess's hand. "Come on, girl, don't just stand there dawdling. They may need you to help serve supper."

As they went through the kitchen, the head cook questioned them, but when Heather mentioned Eunice's name they were allowed to pass. "Such goings on," Heather said as they passed by a pair of scullery maids. "Must be for Queen Rose's coronation dinner."

A maid turned around, glaring at Heather. "Not Queen Rose," she said sharply. "Queen Heather."

Heather struggled to keep her expression under control. First, how could *Heather* possibly be queen? Second, this "scullery maid" used to be Princess Heather's handmaid, Mindy. What was she doing down here? And what was this news of Queen Heather?

"Mindy?" Heather said quietly.

"What?" Mindy blinked. "How do you know me?"

"Come on, Mindy." The other maid handed Mindy a greasy pot. "Quit your grousing and get back to work." She looked at Heather. "Mindy got the sack today, and she's madder than a wet hen. Used to work for Queen Heather, she did, but now she's stuck down here." She laughed. "Just goes to show you."

"Mindy," Heather said again. "Please, take us to see Mrs. Eunice."

"No you don't," the other girl said quickly. "Mindy's got to stay here and—"

"I believe Mrs. Eunice is head of housekeeping." Heather gave the surly servant a chilly look, holding her gaze as the girl's eyebrows rose. "And she has instructed me to bring Mindy with me when I come to meet with her." Heather grabbed the pot from Mindy's hand and thrust it back at the cheeky maid. "Come now, Mindy."

Mindy's face was a mixture of surprise and wonder, but without giving her time to react, Heather linked arms and tugged her away. "Hurry, we must find Eunice."

After a quick search, Heather, with Mindy and Bess in tow, located Eunice and enticed her to take them into the head maid's storage room. Once they were inside, Heather reached over to latch the door, locking them in.

"What is going on here?" Eunice demanded. "I have no time for tomfoolery. This is a busy night and—"

"I am Princess Heather." Heather reached into the neckline of her dress, pulling out the chain with the royal ring attached. "Can I trust you, Eunice?"

Eunice's eyes grew wide. "Princess Heather?"

Heather pulled off her bonnet and held out the ring.

"But you cannot be Queen Heather. She is in the royal chambers dressing for her coronation celebration supper."

"No, that is Princess Rose pretending to be me. I'm afraid she has deceived everyone, and I'm sure she's set the guards out to find me. Possibly to me locked up or worse." Heather knew she was speculating, but Rose's pretense to be Heather, and her plan to receive the crown and usurp the throne, was a serious crime.

"Oh, my word!" Eunice put a hand to her forehead, looking faint.

"Princess Heather," Mindy declared. "I had a feeling something was wrong when you—I mean Princess Rose—told me I was dismissed."

"I'm sorry about that. But I need both of you to help me. What my sister has done must be undone." Heather started to unbutton her bodice, nodding to Eunice. "Bess, Mindy, and I need handmaid's clothes." She pointed to Bess and Mindy. "Get ready to change. After we're properly dressed, we'll carry some fresh linens and things up the servants' stairs. It's so busy that we should go unnoticed. We will go directly to my chambers."

She extracted her key that had been tucked into her chemise and held it up. "In my chambers, you will help me change into the formal gown made for my coronation." She looked down at her dusty plain dress. "It won't do for me to confront my sister looking like a commoner."

"That's right." Mindy touched Heather's hair and frowned. "And we must do something about this. After all, a queen must look like royalty."

"Especially tonight," Bess added.

Mindy beamed at Heather. "Oh, Princess, I'm so glad you're back."

"I'm not fully back," Heather reminded her as Eunice returned with the maids' clothes.

"And not as long as Princess Rose has everyone hoodwinked," Mindy said as they began to dress. "She has managed to convince everyone that she is Queen Heather. I even fell for it. Although something didn't feel right. And then she gave me the sack."

"She sounds like a monster," Bess said as she pulled on the dress.

"How has she explained Princess Rose's absence?" Heather asked.

"She's told everyone Princess Rose is so distraught with grief for the king—" Mindy stopped herself. "Oh, Princess Heather,

I am so sorry for your loss. I nearly forgot. You must be truly brokenhearted about your father's passing."

"I am sad, indeed," Heather admitted as she buttoned the maid's dress. "But, please, tell me more about my sister's doings. I need to be apprised of everything."

"Aye, Princess. As I was saying, your sister is pretending to be you, and she's made everyone believe that Princess Rose is so crushed with grief that she is unable to rise from her bed. Unable to attend any of the festivities. Convenient, I must say."

"What about Sir Edward and Luther?" Heather asked, fearing the answer. "Where are they?"

"Sir Edward arrived before your father's funeral." Mindy shook out a clean white apron. "I saw him for myself. He went to meet with Princess Rose—that was before she began pretending to be you. But he has not been seen since. His wife and Luther have come around, looking for him, but no one knows where he's gone."

Heather cringed to think what her sister might've done to poor Sir Edward. Rose had never been fond of him. "I'm sure the palace is a beehive of activity," Heather said as Mindy helped her tie the apron over the solemn gray maid's dress. "But still we must be cautious when we go out there."

"Oh, another thing," Mindy said as she helped pin the crisp white maid's bonnet onto Heather's artificially grayed hair. "Your sister—rather *Queen Heather*—is engaged, if you can believe it." Mindy turned to help Bess with her bonnet now.

"My sister is engaged?" Heather helped to straighten the bow on Bess's apron strings. "However did that happen?"

"He is a prince from Mandela," Mindy explained. "Not the oldest son, I hear, so he won't inherit the throne. Well, unless he pulls a stunt like your sister has done."

"Mandela?" Heather's eyes grew wide. "What is his name?"

"Prince Michael. Of course, he will attend tonight's dinner and festivities—with *Queen Heather.*" She scowled. "What a mockery."

Heather eased herself down to the wooden bench by the door. "My sister is engaged to Michael?"

"That's correct." Mindy had Bess turn around, checking to be sure she was ready. "Your sister has been busy."

"I should say so." Heather stood, suppressing the vast array of emotions churning away inside her chest. "But we need to keep moving, girls. No time to waste. And we can't all go out there together."

"That's true," Mindy agreed. "That would not look normal."

Heather pressed her lips together as she tried to think. "Mindy, you go first because you know the way." She handed her the basket of fruit that Eunice had brought in as well as the key to Heather's chambers. "And Bess, you will follow Mindy at a reasonable distance." She picked up a stack of clean bed linens, placing them in Bess's arms. And I will come last." Heather looked around the room for something to occupy herself, deciding on a tray with soaps and toiletries. "Here we go," she said.

Waiting for Mindy to go first, Heather counted to ten then told Bess to go. "Keep your eyes on Mindy," she said. "Follow, but not too close. And do not look at anyone else. Imitate how Mindy walks. And don't lose her."

This time Heather counted to twenty. She picked up the toiletries tray and, holding her head high, made her own exit. Fortunately, she would only be passing by servants, but she knew she could not be too careful. And, she hoped, all the important players—the visiting dignitaries and councilmen, and most importantly her conniving sister—would be in their rooms preparing for the night's festivities. Heather didn't even allow herself to imagine where Michael might be right now. How could he have fallen for Rose's deceit?

As angry as she felt at her diabolical sister, her vexation toward Michael was almost equal. She was afraid if she saw Michael and Rose together, she would want to kill them both. It was probably fortunate her weapons had gone missing.

To her enormous relief, Heather made it all the way to her chambers without drawing any attention. There, Bess and Mindy were waiting for her. Mindy had already laid out Heather's fine white gown, and Bess was building a fire to take the chill off the room.

"I'm sorry we don't have a bath or any hot water for you to wash with," Mindy said as she filled Heather's wash basin with water.

"Don't be concerned." Heather set the tray of toiletries down. "I've been washing in rivers and streams for days." She sniffed a bar of lavender soap. "Just having this is luxurious.'

After Heather peeled off the maid's clothes and donned her dressing gown, she did a hasty cleanup, mostly trying to remove the chalky ashes.

"We haven't much time," Heather said as she rubbed some lavender ointment into her hands and face.

"Not if you want to attend the dinner." Mindy pointed to the chair by the dressing table. "Time for your hair."

Heather frowned into the mirror as she sat down. "I hope you can get that out of my hair without having to wash it."

"I have a plan," Mindy assured her. And with Bess watching on, Mindy worked fast, combing and brushing and applying some hair tonic, before she began to style it up onto Heather's head.

"Oh my." Bess's eyes grew wide as she stared at Heather. "I thought you were nice looking for a boy, but you make a beautiful queen."

"Wait until you see her in that gown," Mindy said.

Finally, with her hair gleaming in place and the shimmering white gown on, Heather opened her jewelry box to remove the diamond necklace and earrings that her father had given her to wear with her coronation gown. "These were your mother's," he'd said somberly. "She wore them on our wedding day—when she became my queen. You will wear them when you take the crown." But to her stunned surprise, they were gone.

"I cannot believe it." Heather closed the box and sighed.

"Princess Rose—acting like she was you—insisted on taking my key," Mindy said sadly. "She must've used it to come in here and steal your jewels. I'm sorry."

"Time to confront my sister." Heather stood.

"But I thought you were going to do that at the dinner," Mindy said in alarm. "With everyone there to see."

"I'm afraid that is too much drama. And then everyone would

know what a fool my sister has been, and the kingdom would become a laughingstock."

"Then what do you plan to do?" Mindy looked worried. "Do you realize how dangerous Princess Rose may be? She has guards posted outside the royal chambers. And her staff all around her. There are only three of us."

"That is why you must go downstairs and find our trusted friends." Heather reached for a pen and paper and quickly scribed names of the guards that she knew would come to her aid. "Yes." She looked at the list. "That should be sufficient. Tell them Queen Heather has asked for their assistance. And tell them it's urgent." She checked her clock to see it was already half past seven. "The dinner is supposed to begin at eight. Tell the guards to come directly to the Royal Chambers at a quarter till the hour."

"What about me?" Bess asked after Mindy had gone.

"You shall come with me," Heather told her. "I have need of your assistance."

"Aye, Princess Heather. Whatever you say. I would gladly follow you into battle if you asked me."

Heather smiled. "It may come to something like that, but I hope not."

"What would you have me do?" Bess asked eagerly.

"I suspect you are a strong girl, Bess. You may end up tussling with one of my sister's maids."

Bess grinned. "I would be happy to tussle with your sister herself."

"Leave that to me," Heather said.

"I would gladly die for you," Bess pledged. "I swear that I would."

Heather patted Bess's shoulder. "Thank you. I pray it will not come to that." She took in a deep breath. "And you say a prayer, my friend, that all goes well. It is time to go."

As Heather went to the door, she explained how Bess should walk a couple of steps behind her. "I'm sure we will be watched. Just try to act respectful. I hope my sister hasn't told them to seize me and throw me in the dungeon. If it should come to that, I want you to make a fast exit, and you must find Mindy and let her know."

"Your sister would throw you in the dungeon?"

Heather sighed. "I'm afraid so."

"What a witch." Bess looked embarrassed. "Sorry, Your Highness."

"It's all right." Heather smiled. "When you hear me announce I am Queen Heather, you will know it's time to help me with my sister's maids. I'm sure they will try to interfere with my plan."

"I will do what needs to be done," she promised.

Leading the way out, Heather paused by her sister's chambers as she replayed what Mindy had said earlier. *Princess Rose is so sick with grief, she's unable to rise from her bed.* Well then, Heather would see to that.

# Chapter Twenty-Five

Heather held her head high as she went down one set of stairs and, cutting across a section of the marbled main floor, turned toward the staircase that led to the Royal Chambers. As she passed through the main floor, various servants greeted her—just as they had always done—except that now they called her, "Queen Heather." She did not miss the irony of this.

Some said how glad they were she'd made it safely home, others offered condolences regarding her father's demise, and a few hailed hearty congratulations and blessings on her reign. She wasn't quite sure how they knew it was she and not her sister, but she smiled and returned their greetings, thanking them for their well wishes.

As she started up the stairs, she was amused at how oblivious the people were to the real state of their kingdom. They had no idea that a princess war was raging beneath their noses. And that was how she intended to keep it. She saw no need for drama and exposé. For her father's sake, a man who loved peace, as much as for the kingdom.

Her thoughts were with her father as she made her way down the hall that led to what had once been the king's chambers. It rankled to consider how quickly Rose had commandeered their father's private rooms. Appropriating the space for herself and setting up court in there. But then again, it was Rose. So why expect anything less? Heather glanced over her shoulder to see Bess still following.

She was not surprised to see several guards posted by the door to the royal chambers, although they looked alarmed to see her approaching.

"Good evening," she told them, maintaining a dignified manner. "I am here to see my sister."

"Princess Rose?" one of them said with a puzzled expression.

"That's correct." She stepped past him, reaching for the door. It made no difference to her whether he was inquiring if she were Princess Rose or if she were going to visit Princess Rose. The point was to get inside. Before they could say another word or stop her, she went inside, waited for Bess to join her, then closed and locked the door behind her.

"What?" Her sister's head maid Margot stopped from where she was picking up a tea tray, looking at Heather with a confused expression. "Queen Heather?"

"Yes?" came Rose's voice from behind a curtain as she tried to pass herself off as her sister.

Heather exchanged glances with Bess, who was already moving toward Margot.

Margot tossed an uneasy glance at the curtain behind her. "But I thought you were in your—"

"*I* am Queen Heather." The words barely were out of Heather's mouth before Bess pounced on the maid, pinning her onto the couch and holding her hand over the stunned maid's mouth.

"You will be staying right here for the time being," Bess proclaimed, winking at Heather.

Heather went over to the thick curtains that separated the sitting room from the private section of the Royal Chambers. Even before she opened them, her nose was assaulted by Rose's strong rose-scented perfume. That alone should give Rose's identity away, given that everyone knew that Heather didn't wear any scent stronger than lavender.

Heather pushed open the curtains to see Rose sitting with her back to her. Unaware that she had trespassers, Rose was dressed in a sparkling blue gown that was even more elegant than Heather's coronation gown. No surprises there. Seated at her vanity table, which someone must've moved from her old chambers, Rose was examining her reflection with a look of pure satisfaction.

Alice was just putting the finishing touches on Rose's hair, which was styled more intricately and much higher than Heather's. Another giveaway—if anyone were looking closely. Although Rose could probably make up a story, acting as if Queen Heather had decided to try some new things since she'd been crowned.

And there was the crown, sparkling in all its glory on the vanity table. The crown that Rose had stolen with her lies. Next to the crown was the ivory box that Father had presented to Heather several weeks ago. Rose's neck and ears remained bare, so the diamond necklace and earrings must still be in it.

Rose never saw Heather coming as she streaked across the

room, snatching up the crown and the box then stepping back as Alice let out a startled shriek and Rose leaped to her feet.

"What are you doing in here?" Rose demanded.

"A question I was about to ask you," Heather said calmly.

"Guards!" Rose yelled. "Margot, run and fetch the guards."

"Margot is detained," Heather told her.

Rose looked at Alice. "Go get the guards."

"I wouldn't," Heather said, locking eyes with Alice. "Not unless you relish the idea of spending the rest of your days in the dungeon." Heather stood her ground, blocking Rose from the door. "And I think you know I can do that. I am Queen Heather, and my sister has been playing that she is. But you do know that she's really Rose, do you not?"

Alice nodded nervously. "I know who she is."

"And you know who I am?"

She nodded again.

"You cannot do this," Rose seethed at Heather. "No one will believe you. Besides, you're too late. I have been crowned queen. Ask anyone."

Heather smiled. "Queen Heather has been crowned. Everyone knows that. Already they've been congratulating me, dear sister." Heather leaned down to gaze in the mirror as she put the crown on her head, securing it with pins. And now she held the box out to Alice. "Please, help me with this necklace."

"Don't you dare!" Rose screamed at Alice. "Do not move an inch, or I will have you killed!"

"I command you to do as I said," Heather told Alice. "Am I not your queen?"

Alice nodded, and hurrying over, she grabbed the necklace and arranged it around Heather's neck, fumbling with the clasp.

"Thank you," Heather told Alice. She turned to Rose and shook her head. "I'm so disappointed in you."

"You won't get away with this," Rose seethed at Heather. "I'll go for the Royal Guards myself. They already have my instructions for how to deal with you."

"Stay put," Heather told her. "I mean it."

"You may be able to control my stupid maid, but you cannot control me." Rose glared at Heather as she headed for the curtains. "I'm getting the guards. They will take care of you."

"I promise you, Rose, this will go better for you if you cooperate."

"Guards!" Rose bellowed as she shoved the curtains open. "Yes, you are here!"

Rose was right, the guards had arrived. Not only the ones that had been posted by the door, but the others that Mindy had rounded up too.

"Guards!" Rose commanded with a reddened face. "Take her to the dungeon. At once!"

The guards looked confused, glancing from Rose back to Heather.

"I must apologize for my sister. As you know, she has been out of sorts. And now she is having fits," Heather told the guards. "She got herself dressed and left her chambers, thinking she was well enough to attend the dinner tonight, but as you can see, she is not."

"That's because I am queen," Rose insisted. She rushed toward one of the guards who had been outside her door. "I want you to take this imposter out of here. Throw her in the dungeon. And bring back the crown and the jewels."

"You see what I mean," Heather told a trusted old guard. "Rose is having delusions that she is queen."

"I *am* queen," Rose screamed. "I was crowned yesterday. Everyone saw me crowned."

"Poor Rose." Heather shook her head and sighed.

"But how do we know she's not Queen Heather," one of Rose's guards asked with a sly expression. "Maybe you are just pretending to be the queen."

Heather held out hands that had rarely seen a manicure. "Really? You can't tell by looking at us? Look at Rose's fancy hair. And her gown. And everything about her. She is not me. She is Rose."

"I agree." The old guard nodded. "That is Rose. No doubt about it. I've known her all her life and—"

"Shut up!" Rose screamed at him. "You will be fired immediately." She rushed toward Heather. "Give me my crown, you imposter!"

"Stop right there!" Bess grabbed Rose from behind, keeping her from landing on Heather. "Do not touch the queen."

"I still say we don't know," the corrupt guard said with an evil twinkle in his eye. "Maybe there's been a mix-up. We can't take her word for it just because she's got the crown."

Heather walked over to the old guard, and, reaching into a secret pocket that she'd insisted be sewn into her coronation gown, she pulled out the royal ring. "King Reginald gave this to me before I left on my adventure. He wanted me to have it to prove my identity. But I think everyone in this room knows who I am."

The consensus was in. It was hard to argue with the royal ring. "I want the guards and maids who have corroborated with Rose locked up. And I want Rose locked in her chambers with three trustworthy guards at her door."

"Wait!" Rose yelled out. "I can prove I am Queen Heather. Listen to me!"

Heather gave her sister a disappointed look. "Please, Rose, you must let this go. Or I will have to put you in the dungeon too."

"You all must remember that I am engaged. And Prince Michael can attest to the fact that I am indeed Queen Heather. We were together on my escapade this past week," she said. "If I were gone from the palace, spending time with the Prince of Mandela, I would have to be Heather."

"She makes a good point," one of the guards said.

"Send for Prince Michael," Rose commanded. "At once."

Heather was angry. As much at Michael as she was at her sister. The last person she wanted to see was Michael, the traitor. But for the sake of the kingdom, she must remain calm. "Fine," she told a guard. "Fetch Prince Michael."

Within minutes, Michael was escorted into the Royal Chambers, but when he saw the two sisters standing side by side, he was speechless.

"I see you have met my sister," Heather said to him with impatience.

"He has asked me to marry him," Rose declared, going to Michael's side. "Have you not, my dear?"

Michael blinked, looking between Rose and Heather. "What is this? What is going on?"

"Did Rose not tell you she had a twin?" Heather asked him.

"Rose?" He frowned. "She has been ill. I have not yet met Rose."

"Oh, yes, you have." Heather pointed at her sister. "She is the one on your arm."

Michael stepped away from Rose, staring at Heather with a stunned expression. "I didn't know you had a twin, Queen Heather."

"See, he calls her Queen Heather," the old guard proclaimed.

"But he is engaged to me," Rose argued. "You asked me to marry you, Prince Michael. Don't you remember? What about our kiss?"

Michael looked from Rose to Heather with a sickened look.

"You proposed to my sister," Heather told him. "You asked Rose to marry you yesterday." She glared at him. "And I think that is an excellent solution. It saves me from having to lock her up. If you promise to leave here in the morning and to take her to your kingdom tomorrow, you may marry her tonight."

"No!" Michael crossed his arms across his chest and scowled. "You cannot force me to marry Rose."

"Please," Rose begged him. "Do as my sister says. Marry me tonight and take me to Mandela tomorrow. Please, Michael, do as Queen Heather commands."

"She may be queen of this kingdom," Michael declared, "but she does not rule over me."

Heather stepped closer, looking him in the eye. "I rule over you when you are in my kingdom, Michael."

He frowned. "Fine. That may be true. But you cannot force me to marry your sister."

"Force you? You proposed marriage to Rose. You are the one who kissed Rose. Did someone *force* you to do that?"

The room grew so silent that Heather could hear the clock ticking.

"Yes." Michael spoke quietly. "You did force me, Heather. You may not know it, but when we were together in the wilderness, your spirit and your courage and your beauty, they all forced me to think of you in a whole new way. And after our kiss…well, I knew you were the one. When I proposed marriage to Rose, I thought I was speaking to you. I *never* in a million years would've asked for Rose's hand. And I refuse to marry her now. I would rather be locked up in your dungeon."

At this, Rose threw herself onto the sofa, ranting and crying and behaving nothing like a queen.

Heather looked at the old guard. "Please see that Rose is locked in her chambers. By herself. With guards at the door."

"Yes, Your Majesty." He bowed. He and another guard helped Rose to her feet, dragging her toward the door.

Heather turned to another trusted guard. "And please see that all the guards my sister has corrupted as well as her deceitful maids are placed under lock and key as well. I suppose that means the dungeon." She looked at her sister, who still was fighting against the guards. "I assume that's where you've put Sir Edward. Is that right, Rose?"

"Just shut up!" Rose glared at her.

"I suggest you take her the back way," Heather advised the guards as they went out the door. "And please release Sir Edward while you're down there."

No more questions as to Heather's identity were asked as the trustworthy guards gathered the corrupt ones and escorted them out. Heather turned to Mindy and Bess now. "Go down and get yourself some supper." She handed Mindy her key. "And when you are done, you can go to my chambers."

They thanked her, and after they departed, Heather turned to Michael. "So, what am I to do with you?" she asked in a weary tone.

"Forgive me?"

She sighed. "I will think about it." She laid her arm upon his. "But first you must escort me to the Royal Coronation Dinner. Everyone still believes we are engaged."

"Aren't we?" he asked.

She frowned. "Really? You have the gall to ask me that?"

"I thought it was worth a try."

"We must hasten, Michael. We are already quite late."

He opened the door, waiting for her to pass.

"And truly," she said quietly, "if you do not wish to keep up the appearance of an engagement with Queen Heather, you are free to go. I will not hold you here against your will."

"I am not here against my will." He locked eyes with her. "And

I know that we still have much to talk about. I only hope that you will be willing to listen."

"Oh, yes," she said as they walked down the stairs to where a large, elegant crowd of well-wishers were waiting. "I am willing to listen. And I have a few questions for you as well." Heather waved to the people below as they both went down the stairs.

"Hail to Queen Heather," someone yelled, and several others chimed in.

Heather paused on the last step, holding up her hands to quiet them.

"Please, everyone," she called out, "I want to thank you. But I also wish to say something of importance." She waited as the room grew quiet. "I have learned many lessons this past week. Some were hard lessons, indeed. But I have learned something important in regard to being your queen." She paused, taking in a deep breath. "I believe that the purpose of being queen is not so that my people might serve me, but rather so that I may serve my people. And that is what I intend to do."

"Long live the queen!" a man called out, and several others echoed him.

"My sentiments exactly," Michael whispered in her ear. "Long live the queen."

*They all lived
happily ever after...
Or did they?*

# Note to Readers

I had so much fun writing this fairy-tale adventure story that it was hard to quit where I did. But I want to assure you this is not, by any means, the end of Heather and Rose's adventures.

In the second book, Rose will get her comeuppance. Naturally, Heather will be merciful to her twin, but Rose, being Rose, will push Heather's patience to the limits. Things will get thorny.

And what about that Prince Michael? Is his kingdom still preparing for war? And, truly, is he friend or foe? Because, really, what kind of a guy mistakes his "true love" for her sister?

Heather must determine who she can or cannot trust as she attempts to get to the bottom of these perplexities as well as manage the kingdom, which is in dire need of a firm but gracious hand. Watch for the second book of the Princess Wars series, *A Royal Redemption*, to release in 2024.

CPSIA information can be obtained
at www.ICGtesting.com
Printed in the USA
BVHW031040040423
661729BV00013B/883

9 798887 090153